A Creature of the Night

An Italian Enigma

Fergus Hume

Pharos Books

ISBN: 978-81-19831-45-6
eISBN: 978-81-19831-52-4

©Publisher

Publisher: Pharos Books (P) Ltd.
Plot No.-63, 1st Floor, Main Mother Dairy Road
Pandav Nagar, East Delhi-110092
Phone: 011-40395855, +4049916623
WhatsApp: +91 9319228272
E-mail: sales@pharosbooks.in
Website: www.pharosbooks.in
First Edition: 2024

A CREATURE OF THE NIGHT
Fergus Hume

CONTENTS

TO
GRAHAM PRICE,
IN REMEMBRANCE OF ITALIAN IDLINGS,
SPRING, 1891.

CHAPTER I

THE GHOUL

I think it is Lord Beaconsfield who, in one of his brilliant stories, makes the clever observation that "adventures are to the adventurous," and certainly he who seeks for adventures even in this prosaic nineteenth century will surely succeed in his quest. Fate leads him, chance guides him, luck assists him, and although the adventure supplied by this trinity of circumstances may be neither so dangerous nor so picturesque as in the time of Borgia or Lazun, still it will probably be interesting, which after all is something to be grateful for in this eminently commonplace age of facts and figures. Still, even he who seeks not to prove the truth of Disraeli's aphorism, may, after the principle of Mahomet's mountain, have the adventure come to him, without the trouble of looking for it, and this was my case at Verona in the summer of 18—.

The Cranstons were always a poor family, that is, as regards money, although they certainly could not complain of a lack of ancestors; and when it came to my turn to represent the race, I found that my lately deceased father had left me comparatively nothing. Not having any fixed income, I therefore could not live without doing something to earn my bread; and not having any business capacity, I foresaw failure would be my lot in mercantile enterprise. I was not good-looking enough to inveigle a wealthy heiress into matrimony; and as, after a survey of my possessions, I found I had nothing but a few hundred pounds and an excellent baritone voice, I made up my mind to use the former in cultivating the latter with a view to an operatic career.

Italy, living on the traditions of the days of Rossini, of Donizetti and of Bellini, has still the reputation of possessing excellent singing-masters, so to Italy I went with a hopeful heart and a light purse, and established myself at Milan, where I took lessons, in singing, from Maestro Angello. Milan is a detestable city, hot and arid in summer, cold and humid in winter; and as a year after I arrived in the land of song the end of spring was unusually disagreeable, Maestro Angello went to Verona for a change of air, and thither I followed him with no small pleasure at escaping from that dreary commercial capital of the north which has all the disagreeables of Italian life without any of the compensating advantages of romance and beauty.

But Verona! ah, it was truly delightful, that sleepy town lying so peacefully on the banks of the rapid Adige, dreaming amid the riotous present of the splendid past, when Can Grande held his brilliant court, and received as an honoured guest the great poet Dante, exiled by ungrateful Florence. The city of the gay rhymer Catullus, merry lover of Lesbia, who wept more tears over her sparrow than she did over her poet. The city of Romeo and Juliet, star-crossed lovers as they were, who were recompensed for their short, unhappy lives by gaining immortality from the pen of Shakespeare as types of eternal love and eternal constancy, for the encouragement of all succeeding youths and maidens of later generations. Yes, indeed, with all these memories, historical and poetical, Verona was a pleasant place in which to idle away a summer, so I thanked the kind gods for my good fortune and enjoyed myself.

Not that I was idle. By no means! Maestro Angello kept me hard at work at exercises and scales, so I studied industriously most of the day and wandered about most of the night in the soft, cool moonlight, when Verona looked much more romantic than in the garish blaze of the Italian sun.

It was on one of these nights that an adventure happened to me, an adventure in which I was involved by the merest chance, although I confess that the vice of curiosity had a good deal to do with my entanglement therein.

After dining at the hotel I went out for my customary stroll, and having lighted a pipe as a preventive against the evil odours which seem inseparable from all Italian towns, I wandered on through the deserted streets in a listless, aimless fashion, contrasting in my own mind the magnificent Verona of the past with the dismal Verona of the present. Taken up with these fantastic dreamings, I did not notice particularly where I was going, or how quickly the time was passing, until I found myself on the Ponte Aleardi—that iron bridge which spans the Adige—and heard the church bells chiming the hour of eleven.

The moon was shining in the darkly blue sky amid the brilliant stars, and the leaden waters of the river shone like a band of steel in the pale, silvery light. On either side of the stream lowered dark masses of houses, from the windows of which gleamed here and there orange-coloured lights, while against the clear sky arose the tall steeples of the churches and the serrated outlines of full-foliaged trees. It was wonderfully beautiful, and the soft wind blowing through the night, rippled the swift waters to lines of ever-vanishing white; so leaning over the balustrade of the bridge, I dreamed and smoked, and smoked and dreamed, until the chiming of the half-hour warned me to return to my hotel.

The night, however, was so beautiful and cool, that I could not but think of my hot sleeping-chamber with repugnance, and feeling disinclined for rest, I made up my mind to stroll onward for some time. I might have visited that fraudulent tomb of Juliet in the moonlight, but as I had already seen it by day, and could not feel enthusiastic about such a palpable deception, I refused to be further victimised, and crossed over the bridge to the left shore of the river.

It was somewhat solitary, there, but I was not afraid of robbers, as I had but little money and no jewellery on me, and moreover I felt that, should occasion arise, I could use my fists sufficiently well to protect myself. Being thus at ease regarding my personal safety, I lighted a cigar which luckily happened to be in my pocket, and wandered on until I came within sight, of the cemetery.

Now I firmly believe that every one has in him a vein of superstition which is developed in accordance with his surroundings. Place a man at midday in a bustling city, and he scoffs at the idea of the supernatural; but let him find himself at midnight alone on a solitary moor, with the shadows of moonlight on every side, and all his inherent superstition will start to life, peopling the surrounding solitude with unseen phantoms, more terrible than those of the Arabian Nights. Whether it was the time of night, or the proximity of the burial-ground, I do not know, but I felt my breast fill with vague fears, and hastened to leave the uncanny spot as quickly as possible.

Fate, however, was against me, for in my blind speed, instead of crossing the bridge, I turned to the left, and unexpectedly found myself in the vicinity of another burial-ground. It was apparently much older than the one I had first seen, and there was a ruined wall around it, overtopped by tall, melancholy cypresses, looming black and funereal against the midnight sky. By this time I had recovered my nerve, and feeling somewhat ashamed of my former ignominious flight, I determined to punish myself by entering this antique abode of the dead, and examining it thoroughly.

With this idea I climbed over a portion of the broken wall, and in the shadow of the cypress-trees—shadow dense as the darkness of Egypt—I viewed the mournful scene before me, with mingled feelings of curiosity and dread.

It was evidently very old, for even under the softening light of the moon, the near tombs looked discoloured and time-worn. I saw the soft swell of the green turf, betokening graves, upon which grew the grass long and rank; the milky gleam of slender white columns, broken at the top to typify the short lives of those who slept below; and while yonder, in frowning grey stone, stood a solemn pyramid, built in imitation of those Egyptian monsters by the Nile, here, near at hand, a miniature temple of white marble, delicate and fragile in construction, hinted at the graceful architecture of Greece. Among these myriad tombs arose the slender, lance-shaped cypress-trees, and their dark forms alternating with gleaming crosses of white marble, sombre pyramids, classic temples, and innumerable lines of tall columns, gave to this singular scene the aspect of a visionary city of the dead, which had become visible to mortal eyes by the enchantments of the moon.

Fascinated by the weirdness of this solitude, I let my cigar fall to the ground, and, hidden in the gloom of the cypress-trees, stared long and earnestly at this last abode of the old Veronese, when suddenly my hair bristled at the roots, a cold sweat broke out on my forehead, and a nervous shudder made my frame tremble as if with ague.

The cause of this sudden fear was that, while wrapt in contemplation of this desolate necropolis, I heard a laugh, a low, wicked laugh, which seemed to come from the bowels of the earth. It was now nearly midnight, that hour when the dead are said to come forth and wander among the living, whose nightly sleep so strangely mocks the semblance of that still repose which chains these spectres to their tombs during the day. This idea pierced my brain like a knife, and for the moment, under the influence of the hour, the ghastly scene, the evil laugh, I believed that I was about to witness this terrible resurrection. I tried to turn and fly, but my limbs were paralyzed, and like a statue of stone I stood there rooted to the earth, feeling as if I were under the influence of some horrible nightmare.

Again I heard that wicked laugh, and this time it seemed to come from a tomb near me, a square block of gray stone, in the centre of which was an iron door, evidently the entrance to some vault. Beside this portal stood a life-sized figure in white marble of the Angel of Death, guarding the entrance with a flaming sword, the undulating blade of which seemed, to my startled eye, to waver against the blackness of the door. All round this strange tomb the grass grew long and thick, but, half veiled by the tangled herbage, star-shaped flowers glimmered in the moonlight.

In another moment I would have fled, when for the third time I heard the evil laugh, the iron door of the tomb slowly opened, and a dark figure appeared on the threshold. The sight was so terrifying that I tried to mutter a prayer, feeling at the time as firm a belief in the visitation of the dead as any old woman; but my throat was so dry that I could do nothing but remain silent in my hiding-place and stare at this ghoul, vampire, wraith, or whatever it was, leaving its tomb.

To add to the horror of the situation, the moon had obscured herself behind a thick cloud, and there was now a deep darkness over all the graveyard, a darkness in which I could see nothing, and only hear the faint sigh of the wind, the rustle of the dry grasses, and the loud beating of my heart.

Suddenly I felt that this creature of the night was passing near me, and in abject terror I shrank back against the rough trunk of the tree under which I was standing. I heard nothing in the still night, I saw nothing in the thick darkness; but I felt it pass, by that sixth sense which is possessed by those who have highly strung nerves. In another moment the moon emerged from behind the clouds in all her splendour, and the burst of light gave me courage, for without considering the danger, either material or immaterial, I rushed quickly towards the broken wall, in which direction I judged this unseen ghoul had gone.

The white moonlight flooded the whole space between the burial-ground and the river, so that I saw clearly this figure walking quickly away in the direction of the Ponte Aleardi. It was draped in a long black cloak with a monkish hood, and with its trailing, noiseless garments it seemed to glide along in the moonlight like a shadow.

I had been so quick in my pursuit that it was only a little distance away, and as I peered cautiously over the broken wall it paused for a moment, and, throwing back its hood, looked towards the place where I was hiding. The space between us was so small and the moonlight so lustrous that I could see the face and head plainly rising from amid the dark drapery.

The face was that of a woman, a beautiful woman with full crimson lips, large dark eyes, and great masses of reddish-coloured hair, for even in the cold moonlight I could see the warm, bronze glint of her tresses. One hand, slender and white, clasped the dark robe to her breast, and she looked towards the darkness of the broken wall as if she knew that some one had seen her terrible resurrection. On her delicate features there was a cold, stern look, like that of the ancient Medusa, and truly I felt as if I were turning into stone before the cruel glare of those eyes which seemed to pierce the gloom in which I lay hid. It will be said that I describe somewhat minutely the appearance of this ghoul, seeing that I only beheld her for a moment in the pale, uncertain gleam of the moon; but so close was she to the wall, and so highly strung were my nerves by the weirdness of the situation, that the sudden apparition of this creature of the night photographed itself indelibly on my brain.

At last she seemed satisfied with her gazing at the burial-ground from whence she had emerged, and, again drawing her hood over her face, glided rapidly away towards the Ponte Aleardi. Moved by curiosity and supernatural fear, I determined to follow this spectre and find out where she was going, so without a moment's hesitation I jumped down, and, keeping in the shadow of the wall, stole after her noiselessly and swiftly.

Who was she? Some unhappy ghost of antique Verona, who had committed one of those terrible crimes invented by Lucrezia Borgia, and who was condemned by God to nightly revisit the scene of her former splendour as a punishment for her evil life? Some ghoul who left the feast of the dead in order to prey upon the living? Some vampire, lusting for blood, hastening towards the sleeping city to select her victim and drain him of his life-blood? All the wild, weird tales which I had heard recurred to my memory; all the terrible legends of Brittany, of the East, of Spain, and of the savage North. The memories of witches rifling the dead for their unholy needs, of wizards holding orgies in lonely churchyards, of magicians evoking the silent tenants of the grave by powerful spells, and of demons entering the bodies of the newly dead in order to roam the midnight world—all these gruesome ideas surged in my brain like the delirium of fever.

My fear had passed away. I felt intensely curious to know the errand upon which this woman was bent, and, with all my faculties sharpened by danger, I sped swiftly after this flying spectre, which, looking neither to right nor left, glided rapidly onward towards the sleeping city of Verona.

***

CHAPTER II

A BOCCACCIAN ADVENTURE

Italian towns are very perplexing to strangers. Keep to the principal thoroughfares built in modern days, and you may have a reasonable hope of finding your way about; but once get enmeshed in the crooked, narrow, winding streets of the period of the middle ages and you are lost. The Italians, like Nature, delight in curves, and these narrow alleys, with cobble-stone pavements and no side-walks, dignified by the name of streets, twist in and out, and here and there, between forbidding houses, seven or eight stories in height, under heavy archways, which threaten to fall and crush the unwary stranger, and down steep flights of worn steps, until you become quite bewildered by the labyrinthian windings. Then these houses are built high in order to exclude the burning sun from the alleys, and a cold, humid feeling pervades the entire network of streets; so that what with the gloom, the twistings, and the treacherous pitfalls in dark corners, one feels like Orpheus going down to Hades in search of lost Eurydice.

Having been warned of the difficulty of exploring these unknown depths, I had mostly confined my wanderings to the broad, modern streets and the populous piazzas; therefore as long as my spectre guide kept to the Via Pallone, which begins at the Ponte Aleardi and ends at the Piazza Vittoria Emanuele, I felt quite safe. When, however, after leaving the Piazza she plunged into the narrow streets of the medieval period, I hesitated at first to follow her. I did not know my way, I was a stranger, and unarmed; moreover, I knew not into what unknown dangers I might be led by this mysterious woman who had emerged from the graveyard.

Curiosity, however, prevailed over fear, and as at any moment I might lose sight of her, and thereby never discover if she were of this or the other world, I followed her boldly into the intense gloom into which she had vanished. My eyes could hardly pierce the darkness, and I feared I would not be able to keep her in sight, when luckily a portion of her cloak became disarranged, and I saw the vivid glimmer of a white dress, on which I kept my eyes fastened as a guiding star.

Here and there in the houses lights were burning dimly, but the hour being late, no people were in the streets; and as I followed this noiseless phantom along the solitary alleys, with the dark houses on either hand, and the white gleam of the moonlit sky above, I felt as if I were moving in a dream.

Onward she glided, turning down here, climbing up there, until my feet were weary with walking; and besides, not knowing the way, I stumbled frequently, which gave me many a bruise. The darkness, however, seemed no obstacle to the ghoul, who walked onward as rapidly as if she were still in the moonlight; on the contrary, it was only by the greatest care that I could grope my way sufficiently quickly to keep her in sight, and prevent her from discovering me by my frequent stumbles.

I was about to give up the chase in despair, when suddenly she led me out on to a small square, and hastening across it, disappeared into a palace at the further end. I remained in the alley until she vanished, as I feared if I followed her too closely she might perceive me in the moonlight. The place, which occupied the whole of one side of the square, was a richly decorated building, with a great arched portal in the centre; but I had no time to examine it closely, for, fearful of losing my ghoul, I ran quickly across the square, came to the portal, and was stopped by an iron gate.

It was one of those heavy iron gates common to Italian palaces, which stretching across from wall to wall, afford a view of the inner court, and are only open on festive occasions, or to admit vehicles. I knew that entrance was ordinarily afforded by a side door, and without doubt this was the way she had gone, unless indeed, being supernatural, she found bolts and bars no hindrance. Determined to pursue this strange adventure to the end, I sought the side door, but, on finding it, discovered to my vexation that it was locked. I could not enter that way, and the bars of the iron gate were so close together, that a man of my size could not possibly squeeze through them, so to all appearances the adventure, as far as I was concerned, was finished.

Making one last effort, however, I felt all the iron bars singly, to see if any one was loose, in which case I could remove it and thus slip through; when to my astonishment, on the left side of the gate furthest from the door, I found that one of the bars had been wrenched away. Without waiting to consider this, which was curious to say the least of it, I concluded that the woman, if indeed she were flesh and blood, had entered by this breach in the gate, so at once took advantage of my discovery and soon found myself in the courtyard. The palace appeared to be quite deserted, as the windows were all broken, and the ironwork of the balconies which ran round the four sides of the courtyard, at different heights, was twisted out of all shape; besides which, the mosaic pavement upon which I stood was smashed in several places, and grass grew between the interstices. I could see all this plainly in the moonlight, and, moreover, as a great door at the end of the courtyard opposite the iron gate was slightly ajar, while all the other smaller doors were closed, I came to the conclusion that the ghoul had gone in there. My conjecture proved correct, for as, hiding in the shadow, I peered into the gloom of the building, I saw the sudden flare of a torch which the woman had just fired, and with this in her hand she began to climb up a flight of steps—at least, so I judged from seeing the torch rise higher and higher in the darkness until it vanished altogether.

The lightning of the torch made me believe that I had to do with flesh and blood, as certainly no phantom would use natural ways and means in preference to supernatural; so directly the light disappeared, I stole cautiously across what appeared to be a large hall, grasping my walking-stick tightly in case of any surprise. I could not disguise from myself that my curiosity had led me into a very perilous adventure,

A Creature of the Night

but, as since the affair of the torch I had quite recovered my nerve, I went resolutely forward, and, feeling my way carefully in the dark, climbed up the staircase.

At the first turning of the ascent all was still in darkness, but on taking the second turning I saw the torch gleaming like a fierce yellow star in the gloom of a long corridor. Luckily I had very light, thin shoes on, and trod cautiously, otherwise the echo of my footsteps would most surely have betrayed me to the mysterious torch-bearer. The palace was certainly not inhabited, as I heard nothing to support such a belief; but as I hastened along the wide corridor, through the windows on the left side streamed the pale moonlight, and I saw that the glass in these windows was painted to represent coats-of-arms, so without doubt this deserted mansion had once been the residence of some great Veronese noble.

But what was the ghoul doing here? Why had she come from her vault in the churchyard to this neglected habitation? Again the fear seized me that this creature was a phantom of some splendid lady of the middle ages, come to revisit the scenes or her antique magnificence. The cold air as I passed along seemed full of the strange perfume of sandalwood, and this sensuous odour in conjunction with the flitting torch, the coloured shadows cast on the floor by the moonlight streaming in through the painted windows, and the state of nervous excitement in which I was, all made me feel like the hero of one of those amorous adventures which are described in the glowing pages of Boccaccio.

Once more the torch disappeared round a corner to the left, but in a moment I had it again in sight; another flight of shallow steps, another short corridor, and at the end an arched door, through which the phantom disappeared. At the door I paused to consider what I should do next, as, if I rashly entered the room, I might pay for my temerity with my life; so I stood irresolutely at the half-open door, ready to fly at the least sign of danger.

As I stood at the door in the intense gloom, for there were no windows in this corridor, I saw a faint glimmer of light in the room within, and this light remaining stationary for some considerable time, I judged that the lady of the sepulchre had left the torch there and retired into some inner chamber. Resolving, therefore, to risk the attempt, I peered into the apartment, and saw the torch stuck in a socket made in a small table in the centre of this small hall, which was hung with ancient tapestry. At the end opposite the portal through which I was looking, was an opening draped with heavy red curtains embroidered with gold, for every now and then as they stirred I saw the dull glitter of the tarnished metal.

Determined not to be discovered, I thought it a capital plan to hide between the tapestry and the wall, so as to secure good concealment, and then steal along the walls until I arrived at the curtained opening, through which I hoped to be able to see into the room beyond. Just as I made up my mind to put this plan into practice, the torch, which had been burning very low, flickered and went out, so that the hall was in complete darkness. In the gloom, however, rays of bright light shone through the embroidered curtains. I heard the murmur of voices, and then the sharp, clear notes of a mandolin. The ghoul evidently had some one with her, perhaps the unfortunate individual whom she proposed to devour; so as no time was to be lost, I slipped into the apartment, enconced myself between the tapestry and the wall on the left of the door, and prepared to creep along, if possible, to the curtained archway. While I paused a moment to regain breath and courage, for certainly the situation was not without an element of danger, the metallic notes of the mandolin ceased and a man's voice began singing some Italian song, but one with which, in spite of my knowledge of music, I was not acquainted. It was a slow and sensuous melody of passionate sweetness with an undercurrent of sadness, and the singer had a remarkably fine tenor voice, sounding full and rich even through the heavy curtains, which prevented me hearing the words clearly. Evidently this was an amorous rendezvous, but why was it taking place in this deserted palace, and why had the lady come from a vault in a graveyard to keep it?

All at once the singer stopped abruptly in the middle of a phrase, I heard the mandolin suddenly smashing on the marble floor, and then sounded the low, wicked laugh I had first heard at the burial-ground. Filled with anxiety to learn the meaning of all these strange events,

I glided rapidly along the wall, and speedily arrived at the curtained opening. Being afraid to pull it to one side lest I should be discovered, I took out my penknife and made a slit in the heavy embroidery; then, looking through the opening thus obtained, I beheld a most extraordinary spectacle.

A circular chamber, not very large, but very lofty, surrounded by eight half-pillars of veined white marble built into the wall, and supporting a domed ceiling richly painted with garlands of flowers, from amid which peered the smiling faces of beautiful women. Between these noble pillars hung voluminous draperies of darkly red velvet, all magnificently embroidered with fantastic designs in tarnished gold thread, but, curiously enough, the apartment had no windows, neither in the ceiling nor at the sides, so whatever took place within could not be seen save through the curtained archway.

In the centre of the white marble floor stood a low, heavy table, richly gilt, and covered with the remains of a splendid feast. The gorgeousness of the vessels thereon was truly marvellous, consisting, as they did, of elaborately chased silver epergnes filled with brilliantly-coloured fruits; many-branched candelabra of gold, bearing slender wax tapers to illuminate the apartment; gracefully carved jugs, of wonderful designs which must have emanated from the brains of Cellini himself; and strangely shaped antique goblets which put me in mind of the sacramental cups used in Italian churches at the celebration of the mass. The voluptuous scent of sandalwood pervaded the heavy atmosphere of the chamber; gold and silver and crystal shone in the mellow light of the myriad tapers, and the whole appearance of this sensuous banquet was like those of former ages presided over by Can Grande or splendour-loving Cæsar Borgia. I thought I was in dreamland, the more so when I saw the bizarre costumes worn by the two occupants of the room.

One was the lady I had followed from the graveyard, who, having thrown off her heavy cloak, now appeared in a white silk dress of antique cut, richly embroidered with gold. Round her slender neck she wore an old-fashioned necklace of superb rubies, set in silver, which flashed forth crimson flame with every heave of her snowy bosom, while strings of soft-shining pearls were twisted in her magnificent red hair; an Eastern girdle of gold fretwork encircled her waist, and broad gold bracelets radiant with gems clasped her milk-white arms. The profusion of jewels she wore scintillated, with her every motion, throwing out sparks of many-coloured fire, and she looked like one of those proud dames of Venice who smile so haughtily in the pictures of Titian. But her face! Oh, heavens! what a beautiful, cruel, relentless face!—the tigerish look in the splendid eyes, the wicked laugh of the full red lips! Was she truly a woman, or some fiend sent upon earth to lure men to hell by the fascination of her evil beauty?

If the woman was curiously dressed for modern days, her companion, a handsome young man of seven-and-twenty was still more so, as he wore a doublet of pale-blue velvet slashed with white satin and diapered with gold embroidery; a small ruff round his neck; high riding-boots of black leather, reaching to the thigh, with gilt spurs; and a short mantle of azure silk, which drooped gracefully from his shoulders. He had no rapier, but at his girdle hung a small poniard, the handle of which was thickly encrusted with gems, and on the velvet-covered chair beside him lay a large cloak and a small mask of black velvet. I rubbed my eyes and pinched myself to see if I were really awake, for the whole fantastic scene looked like one of those which had doubtless taken place at Verona in the opulent days of her splendour.

"I am mad, asleep, or intoxicated," I thought, as I looked at this Boccaccian feast, at these Boccaccian lovers. "What does it mean? This must be the phantom of Lucrezia Borgia, who has risen from the tomb to meet one of her dead lovers and renew for a time the joys of the past. Oh! I am mad or asleep. I will wake up and find this is all a dream—some fantasy of the brain created by the delirium of fever!"

Between the lovers lay the broken mandolin, and the woman, pointing to this, talked volubly while the young man stood listening with a scornful smile on his lips. Not being a very good Italian scholar, I could not follow all this rapid talk without great difficulty, but from what I could gather it seemed to me that the phantom of Lucrezia Borgia was accusing her lover of infidelity. At length, when she seemed exhausted, he caught up his mantle and mask as if about to go, but she fell prostrate before him, and seemed to implore him to stay. He shook his head, and then springing to her feet in anger, she snatched the poniard from his belt and tried to strike him. The young man warded off the thrust with his left arm, round which was wrapped his heavy black cloak, whereupon she let the dagger fall and began to beseech him again. I could not understand the meaning of this terrible dumb-show any more than I could the curious dresses, the antique chamber or the deserted palace. It was the phantasmagoria of a dream seen by the soft light of the tapers, and my brain being quite upset by the strange events of the night, I entirely forgot the nineteenth century, and seemed to live, to breathe, to tremble, on the threshold of one of those fatal chambers wherein the Medici, the Scaligers and the Borgias feasted, loved, betrayed, and slew their friends, their lovers, and their enemies.

The woman, evidently seeing it was useless, stopped beseeching the young man, upon which he picked up his dagger, and throwing the fold of his cloak over his right shoulder, advanced towards the door without saying good-bye to the lady. I withdrew quickly, fearful of discovery, when, just as his hand was on the curtains, her voice sounded once more slow and deliberate, so that I was able to understand what she said:—

"So you leave me for ever?"

"Yes!" he replied with the same deliberation, "for ever."

"Then before you go, let me drink to your future happiness."

"With pleasure, madame."

He appeared to hesitate at first, but after saying these words I heard him move away from the curtain, upon which I looked again and saw him standing by the chair, while the woman, with her face turned away, was filling a goblet with wine. Her back was towards him, so that he could not see what she was doing, but I could perceive her least action. She filled two goblets with wine, then taking something from her breast, dropped it into one of them, and, turning round with a smile, presented the cup to him. It flashed across me that she was trying to poison her lover, and I would have called out to warn him, but the extreme peril of my position, the terrible appearance of this woman, and the uselessness of interference kept me silent during this supreme moment.

The young man took the cup she gave him, and drained it with a bow, while she simply touched her lips with the other goblet, and smiled again.

"To your future happiness," she said in a significant voice, and set the goblet down on the table.

They talked together after this reconciliation for some time and seemed better friends than before, but I saw that the woman kept furtively glancing at his face with a wicked smile on her lips. At length he handed her the mask, which evidently did not belong to him, and, after kissing her hand, was about to turn in the direction of the archway, when suddenly he grew pale, put his hand to his head quickly, and grasped the chair near which he stood to keep himself from falling.

"Why, what is this?" he cried in a hoarse, strained voice. "Gran Dio! what does it mean?"

She bent forward with a wicked laugh, and the rubies flashed forth venomous red flame in the soft light.

"It means that you have betrayed me and I have revenged myself!"

He looked at her with a dazed expression, made a step forward as if to kill this terrible woman, who, dangling the mask in her hand, stood mocking at his agony with a cruel smile, then suddenly flung up his hands with a wild cry of despair and fell at her feet—dead.

"Fool!" she said, without displaying the least sign of emotion. "Fool!"

I wished to rush forward and denounce the demon in woman's shape who had so vilely perpetrated this cold-blooded murder, but, overcome with horror, I reeled away from the curtain and fell—fell into the arms of some one who held me with a powerful grip. I gasped with alarm and was about to call out, when I felt a handkerchief dashed suddenly over my face wet with some liquid. In spite of my struggles it was held firmly there, and I gradually felt my senses leave me until I knew no more.

* * *

When I came to myself it was early morning, and I was seated on a stone bench in the Piazza Vittoria Emanuele, surrounded by a group of curious onlookers.

"Where am I?" I asked in English.

No one answered, and I repeated the question in Italian, upon which a fat woman spoke up,—

"Signor, you are in the Piazza Vittoria!" she said in a husky voice; "we found you here when we came first."

"But the palace, the woman, the poison!" I said stupidly, for my head was aching terribly.

The peasants looked at one another with a meaning smile and shook their heads. I saw that they thought I had been drinking, so, giving a piece of money to the fat woman who had spoken, I took my way at once to my hotel, which I reached in a state of bewilderment better imagined than described.

***

CHAPTER III

THE FEAST OF GHOSTS

Was it a dream? Common-sense said "Yes." My bruises said "No!" But certainly the whole affair was most remarkable, and quite out of the ordinary kind of events which take place in this prosaic nineteenth century. We have done with those romantic episodes in which the heroes and heroines of Boccaccio, Le Sage and M. Dumas père take part, and in the searching light of the Press lantern, which is nowadays turned on all things and on all men, it is impossible to encounter those strange events of the middle ages. Judging from my experiences of the previous night I had been entangled in a terrible intrigue, which might have taken place under Henri Trois or Lorenzo di Medici, yet, as the past can never become the present, the whole affair was a manifest anachronism. I was inclined to think that I had been the sport of some Italian Puck, but as there are no fairies nowadays, such an idea was absurd, so the only feasible explanation of the bizarre occurrence was that I had been dreaming.

I had certainly gone to the old burial-ground and had seen the phantom of Lucrezia Borgia emerge from an old Veronese tomb, and as certainly I had followed her to the Piazza Vittoria Emanuele, but here, without doubt, reality ended and fiction began. Evidently I had sat down upon the stone bench where I was discovered by the peasants, and had there fallen asleep to undergo this extravagant adventure in a vision of the night. In sleep I had dreamed a dream after the fashion of the Athenian lovers in Shakespeare's comedy, and the antique chamber, the quaint costumes, and the phantom characters had been idle visions of the brain, which had played their several parts in this mediæval phantasmagoria.

To put entirely to one side the impossibility of living people dressing themselves in rococo costumes in order to play a fantastic comedy-tragedy in a deserted place, if I had really seen all I imagined, how did I find myself in the Piazza Vittoria Emanuele at daybreak? The visionary pursuit of the lady of the sepulchre had been a long one, and I certainly could not have walked back such a distance to the Piazza without knowing something about it. But memory ceased at my fainting at the door of the fatal chamber, and revived on my finding myself on the stone bench in the Piazza; therefore, granting that the whole adventure had actually occurred, how had I been taken from the deserted palace to the Piazza?

Idling over my midday meal at the Hotel d'Este, I thought of the extraordinary series of events in which I had taken part, and kept puzzling my brain as to whether they had really occurred or whether I had been the victim of a grotesque nightmare. I had received a letter from the Maestro Angello, saying he could not give me my usual lesson, therefore I determined to devote the whole day, which was thus at my disposal, to finding out the truth or falsehood of this mysterious adventure.

My bruises were very painful, but I doctored myself as I best could, so that without much difficulty I was able to walk. Doubtless I had received these bruises whilst pursuing the unknown from the graveyard to the Piazza Vittoria Emanuele, and thus far I was certain of the actuality of my adventure. With this idea in my head, I made up my mind to go to the old graveyard and discover, if possible, who was buried in the tomb from which the ghoul had emerged. By finding out the name I might possibly ascertain that of the lady, as there must certainly have been some connection between her and the person buried in the mysterious vault. No sooner had I thus sketched out my plan of action than I put it at once into execution, and as I found some difficulty in walking, I sent for Peppino's fiacre in order to drive to the cemetery.

Peppino was a merry little Florentine, whose services I employed for two reasons, one being that he spoke excellent Italian, so that I understood him easier than I did the general run of these Northern Italians, who usually gabble a vile patois which no Englishman can understand without constant practice, and my acquaintance with the modern Latin tongue was not sufficient to warrant my indulging in liberties with it; the other reason was that Peppino, having lived a long time in Verona, knew the town thoroughly, and would be able to tell me better than any one if such a deserted palace as I had dreamed of really existed; besides which, he was also a very amusing companion.

The fiacre duly arrived, and on going outside I found Peppino grinning like a small black monkey as he held the door open for me to enter.

"Dio!" said Peppino in a commiserating tone, seeing how I leaned on my stick, "is the Signor not well?"

"Oh, yes! quite well, Peppino, only I fell yesterday and hurt myself, so you see I have to get you to drive me to-day."

"Bene!" replied Peppino philosophically, mounting the box, "the ill of one is the good of another. To where, Signore?"

"To the cemetery near the Porto Vittoria."

"The new or the old one, Signore?"

"The old cemetery!"

Peppino cast a queer look at me over his shoulder, and, muttering something about the "mad English," drove away towards the Via Pallone. As he was on the box-seat, and the fiacre made a good deal of noise going over the rugged stone pavement, in addition to the incessant jingling of the bells, I could not question him as I desired to do, so, making up my mind to wait until I arrived at the graveyard, I leaned back in the carriage and gave myself up to my own thoughts.

Then a curious thing occurred which made me certain that the events of the previous night had actually taken place, for without the least effort of memory on my part the strange melody sung by the young man in the palace came into my head. I could not possibly have dreamed that, and I could not possibly have composed the air, so I concluded that I had really heard the song, and, having an excellent musical ear, it had impressed itself on my memory. Of course I did not recollect the words, but only the tune, and thinking it might prove useful as a link in the chain of circumstances, I hummed it over twice or thrice so as to keep it in my mind.

I therefore concluded from this piece of evidence that I had actually been to the deserted palace and witnessed that strange feast, but if so, how had I found myself at dawn in the Piazza Vittoria Emanuele? It was no use puzzling my brains any more over this mysterious affair, so the wisest plan would be to wait until I found out the name on the tomb, and then perhaps Peppino would be able to tell me about the palace, in which case, with these two facts to go on, I might hope to discover the meaning of these extraordinary events.

Meanwhile the fiacre had left the Via Pallone, crossed over the Ponte Aleardi, and was now being driven rapidly along the left bank of the Adige, past the Campo Marzo. We speedily arrived at the old burial-ground, and Peppino, stopping his horse near the gate, assisted me to alight from the carriage.

"Peppino," I said, when this was done, "tie your horse up somewhere and come with me into the cemetery."

"Diamine!" replied Peppino, crossing himself with superstitious reverence. "I like not these fields of the dead."

"It's broad daylight, you coward; besides, I wish you to tell me about the tombs."

"But why does not the Signor go to the beautiful new cemetery?" said Peppino, leading his horse to the wall and fastening him to a heavy stone; "the statues there are beautiful. This is old, very old; no one is buried here now."

"When was the last person buried, Peppino?"

"Dio! I don't know—eh, oh, yes, Signore, last year an illustrious was buried in his own vault; but he was mad. Ecco!"

"Why did he have a vault built in such an old cemetery?"

"Oh, the vault was old—as old as the Trezza. All the signori of his family had been buried there for many days."

"Since the Republic?"

"Dio! yes, and before."

"What is the name of this family?"

"I don't know, Signore, I forget!"

"Well, come along, Peppino. As you know so much about one tomb, you will probably know something about another."

"Command me, Illustrious."

I did not enter the burial-ground by the gate, as I wanted to go the same way as on the previous night, in order to be certain of finding the tomb I was in search of, so, with some little difficulty, and the help of Peppino, I managed to climb over the broken wall, and soon found myself in my old hiding-place. Peppino looked at me with considerable curiosity, as he could not conceive my object in coming to this dreary locality; but ultimately, shrugging his shoulders, he put it down to a freak on the part of a mad Englishman, and waited for me to speak.

The tomb looked scarcely less forbidding and gloomy in the daytime than it did at night, with its massive-looking architecture, and the stern-faced angel guarding the iron door. Advancing through the long grass which grew all round it, I looked every where for a name, but could find none, then tried to open the iron door, to the great dismay of Peppino.

"Signore," he said in a faltering voice, "do not let out the ghosts."

"There are no ghosts here, Peppino. They have all departed," I replied, finding the door locked.

"Dio! I'm not so sure of that, Illustrious. Many dead are in there."

"Oh, they've been dead so long that their ghosts must have grown weary of this gloomy sepulchre."

"Yes, Signore, but the ghost of the mad Count buried last year!"

"Oh!" I cried with lively curiosity, "is this the vault where he was buried?"

"Yes, Illustrious!"

"And the name, Peppino? What was his name?"

The little Italian looked perplexed, as he could not understand the interest I took in this sepulchre; still, seeing I was in earnest, he tried to think of the name, but evidently could not recall it.

"Cospetto! Signore, I have the memory of Beppo, who forgot the mother who bore him; but the name will be here, Illustrious, for certain."

"See if you can find it, Peppino," I replied, sitting down on a stone near the iron door. "I am anxious to know to whom this tomb belongs."

Peppino, being more conversant with Italian tombs than myself, went to look for the name, and in a wonderfully short space of time came back with a satisfied smile on his face.

"Signore, the tomb is that of the Morone."

"The Morone?"

"Yes, Signore, they were a great family of Verona, as great as the cursed Medici of my beautiful Florence."

"And this Count, who died last year, was their descendant?"

"Dio! Illustrious, he was the last of them. No father, no brother, no child. He was the last. Basta, basta!"

"Had he a wife?" I asked, thinking of the woman who had emerged from this tomb.

"Yes, Signore, a beautiful wife, but when he died she left Verona for Rome I heard. She is not now here."

Well, I had found out the name of the family buried in the tomb, and that the wife was the sole representative of the race, so I naturally thought she was the only person who would have been able to enter the tomb; although why she did so, unless it was to pray beside the corpse of her late husband, I could not understand. Besides, Peppino, who was one of the greatest gossips in the town, said she had left Verona, so perhaps the midnight visitor was not the Contessa Morone at all.

"Were the Count and Countess an attached couple, Peppino?"

The Italian shrugged his shoulders.

"Dio! I know not indeed," he replied carelessly; "the Signor Conte was certainly mad. I saw him at times, and he had the evil eye. Diamine! often have I made horns for that eye, Illustrious."

"And the Countess, Peppino? Have you ever seen the Countess?"

"No, Signore! The Conte let her not out. Ah! he was jealous, that madman. He was old and the Signora was young. Per Bacco! the husband was afraid of the handsome officers. Ecco!"

A mad and jealous husband, old, too, into the bargain. With such a trinity of imperfections a young and beautiful woman could hardly be much in love with him, and, a year after his death, would certainly not have taken the trouble to pray at his tomb. No! the unknown lady could not possibly have been the Contessa. Who, then was this mysterious visitant? I had now quite got over my fancy that she was a spectre, and felt profoundly curious to find out who she was, and why she had come to this ancient burial-place at midnight.

"Is there a Palazzo Morone, Peppino?"

Peppino changed colour.

"What do you know of the Palazzo Morone, Signore?"

"Oh, there is one then!"

"Yes, Illustrious! It is haunted!"

"Haunted! Nonsense!"

"Dio! Signore, I speak the truth. No one has lived there for the last two hundred years. It is shut up for the rats and the owls and the spectres of the tomb."

"What tomb—this one?"

"Ah, Signore, do not jest, I pray you, or the illustrious Signori Morone will hear us."

Peppino looked so serious that I forebore to smile at this absurdity, lest I should offend his pride and thus lose the story.

A Creature of the Night

"Well, Peppino, tell me all about this haunted palace."

"Not here, Signore, I am afraid!"

"Then help me back to the carriage."

He obeyed with great alacrity, and, when I was once more in the fiacre, prepared to loosen his horse.

"No, no! Peppino," I said, smiling; "the ghosts can't hear us here, so tell me the story of the Morone."

Peppino cast a doubtful glance in the direction of the burial-ground, and then, seating himself on the step of the carriage, began his story. His Italian, as I have said before, was very good, so, making him speak slowly, I was easily able to understand the strange legend he related.

"Signore," he began, with a solemn look on his usually merry face, "the Morone were very famous in Verona four hundred years ago. Dio! they fought with the Scaligers, and afterwards with the Visconti. They were Podestas of the city before the Della Scala, and several of them were great Cardinals. One would have been his Holiness himself, but the Borgia asked him to supper and he died of their poison. About two hundred years ago Mastino Morone wedded the Donna Renata della Moneta, who was said to have been descended on the wrong side from Donna Lucrezia herself."

"You mean that this Renata was an illegitimate descendant of Lucrezia Borgia?"

"Yes, Signore. Ah! she was a devil of a woman, that Madonna Lucrezia. Ebbene! Signore. This Donna Renata wedded with Count Mastino Morone, and a pleasant life she led him, for she loved all other men but him. Cospetto! he would have strangled her, but he was afraid of her many lovers. There was a room in the Palazzo Morone, without any windows, where Donna Renata supped with those she favoured."

"And the room is there still?" I said, thinking of that mysterious chamber.

"Of a surety, Signore! It is haunted by the ghost of the Marchese Tisio!"

"Who was he?"

"Signore, he was the last lover of Donna Renata, whom she killed with the Borgia poison because he was faithless. Eh! it is true, Illustrious. She found out by her spies that the Marchese loved another, so she asked him to a last feast in her room, and when he was going she gave him a cup of wine. Dio! he drank it, the poor young man, and died. Ecco!"

"And why was he her last lover? Did she repent?"

"No, Signore! The Count Mastino was watching at the door, and when she had killed the Marchese he went in to see her."

"And killed her, I suppose?"

"Per Bacco! Signore, no one knows. She never came out of that room again. The friends of the poor Tisio found his body, but they never found Donna Renata."

"Then what became of her?"

"Cospetto! No one ever found out. Mastino married again and said nothing, but after that last feast his first wife was never seen again. Diamine! it is strange."

"It's a curious story, Peppino, but it does not explain how the palace is haunted."

"Listen, Illustrious! I will tell," said Peppino in a subdued whisper. "The spirits of the Donna Renata, of the Conte Mastino, and of the Marchese Tisio, haunt the palace, and in the Month of May, when the crime was committed, the lovers hold a feast in that secret room while the husband watches at the door. Then the Donna Renata poisons the Marchese, the husband enters, and cries of pain and terror are heard. Then the lights go out and all is still."

It was certainly very curious, for Peppino was describing the very same I had beheld—the terrible Renata, the unhappy lover, and the poisoned cup, but the Count——

"Tell me, Peppino, has any one ever beheld this feast of ghosts?"

"Dio! Signore, the people who lived in the palace were so afraid of the ghosts, that they left altogether, and no one has lived there for two hundred years."

"Yes, yes! but this spectral banquet seems all imagination—no one has seen it?"

"Yes, Signore. A holy Frate, who did not fear the devil, went one night in May and saw the feast through the door, but just as the poisoned cup was given, the ghost of the Conte dragged him away and tried to kill him."

"Oh! and did the ghost succeed?"

"No, Illustrious! The Frate made the sign of the cross and called on the Madonna, on which the ghosts all vanished with loud cries, and the Frate fainted. Next morning he found himself——"

"In the Piazza Vittorio Emanuele?"

"No, Signore; lying on the floor of the palace."

I was somewhat disappointed at this different ending to the narrative of Peppino, but it was very extraordinary that my adventure and that of the Frate should be so similar. It was broad day, I had overcome my superstitious fancies, yet the whole affair was so strange that I could not help feeling a qualm of fear, which I tried to laugh off, a proceeding which mightily offended Peppino.

"Signore, it is the truth I tell."

"Suppose I prove it, Peppino. This is the month of May, and no doubt the feast takes place every night. You will show me the palace, and I will watch at the door of the secret room."

"Dio! do not think of it, Illustrious," cried Peppino in alarm; "the Frate himself, a holy priest, was nearly killed, and you, Signore, you are a heretic."

"And, therefore, liable to be carried off by his Satanic Majesty. You are complimentary, Peppino. Nevertheless, to-morrow you must show me the palace."

"The Illustrious must excuse me."

"And watch with me for this feast of ghosts."

"Dio? the Signore jests!"

"No, indeed, Peppino! I am in sober earnest. We will go to the Palazzo Morone to-morrow; and now drive back to my hotel, as I feel very tired. Your story has been very entertaining, nevertheless."

"Ah! the Signor does not believe me?" said Peppino, getting on the box again.

"Yes, I do, Peppino; but I believe your ghostly party can be explained away."

***

CHAPTER IV

THE ANGELLO HOUSEHOLD

The bruises I had received during my nocturnal adventure turned out to be worse than I expected, especially one on the left knee-cap, which quite incapacitated me from walking; therefore I was forced to remain in the house all day. This was somewhat annoying, as I was anxious to find out the Palazzo Morone, and see the chamber of Donna Renata during daylight. I thought also that as the palace bore such an evil reputation, my lady of the sepulchre would think herself safe in leaving the dead body of the young man lying in the room, and if I discovered the corpse I intended to give notice to the authorities of the crime I had seen committed.

Unluckily, however, I had to remain in bed most of the day, and when Peppino came in to say that his fiacre was at the door I was obliged to send him away, much to his gratification, as he was by no means anxious to guide me to the haunted palace. The curious resemblance between my own experience and the legend related by Peppino had rather startled me; but, being certain that I had to deal with the natural, and not the supernatural, I was firmly resolved to unravel this mystery before leaving Verona. To do this every moment was of value, and I bitterly regretted that my stiff knee kept me confined to the house. Everything, however, is for the best, and before I saw the Palazzo Morone, fresh light was thrown upon the events of the night in a most unexpected manner.

After my one day of enforced idleness I was fully determined to seek the conclusion of my adventure the next, when on the following morning I received a note from Maestro Angello, asking me to be sure and come to my lesson. As the Maestro was always annoyed at the non-appearance of a pupil, I judged it wise to go, and arranged with Peppino to search for the Palazzo Morone in the afternoon. The lesson would only last an hour, and I would thus have plenty of time to carry out my intention, as Peppino, knowing the palazzo, would be able to take me there direct.

I felt much better this second day after my adventure, as the pain had quite left my knee, so having thus arranged my plans for the afternoon, I started in a very contented frame of mind for the Casa Angello.

It was a dreary day, for there are dreary days even in Italy, and at intervals there fell heavy showers, which made me feel somewhat depressed. Pedestrians were hurrying along with large umbrellas of the Gamp species, red being the prevailing colour; and what with the sloppy streets, the gloomy houses, and the absence of the chattering Italian populace, the whole place looked infinitely melancholy, so in order to keep up my spirits I hummed the weird air I had heard in the Palazzo Morone.

Maestro Angello lived in a narrow street more like a drain than anything else, and I entered into a damp courtyard through a dismal little tunnel barred by an iron gate. The portinaia, who lived in a glass-fronted room as if she were a unique specimen of the human race preserved in a case, nodded her head to intimate that the Maestro was at home, so I climbed up the evil-smelling stone stairs which went up the side of the courtyard, and soon arrived at Angello's door. Ringing a little bell which tinkled in a most irritating manner, I was admitted into the dingy ante-chamber by Petronella, a short, fat, good-natured woman who managed the whole household, and made a great deal of noise over doing so. She was dressed in an untidy print gown, with a bright red shawl over her shoulders, and wore wooden clogs which clattered noisily on the terra-cotta floor. Her plenteous hair was roughly twisted into a knot and stuck through with large brass pins, which gave her a spiky appearance about the head. This curious apparition saluted me with a jolly smile in a gruff voice, with the usual familiarity of Italian servants,—

"Sta bene! Signore. Ah, the Maestro! povero Maestro!"

"What's the matter with him, Petronella?"

"Eh! Signore, he cannot live much longer."

As Angello was considerably over eighty years of age I thought this highly probable, but was about to condole with Petronella over his illness, when she saved me the trouble of a reply by bursting out into a long speech delivered with much dramatic effect:—

"It is nothing but trouble, Signore. Such a fine young man, and the piccola loved him so! It will surely place the Maestro among the saints. Four masses for his soul, Signore; and those priests are such thieves. I said 'No lesson,' but the Maestro is a mule for having his own way. Let him teach, say I; it will divert his mind! There, Signore, go in with you! But I always thought it would come; four times I heard the cock crowing, a bad sign, as Saint Peter knew. There, there! the Madonna aid us!"

Not understanding in the least what Petronella was talking about, I allowed myself to be pushed mechanically into the inner room in a state of bewilderment. The Maestro, seated in his usual chair, was waiting for me, and his granddaughter, Bianca, who assisted him in his lessons, was looking out of the window at the falling rain. An atmosphere of sadness seemed to pervade the dull, grey room, and as Bianca advanced to meet me I saw that her eyes were red with crying, while old Angello stared at her in a listless, indifferent manner, being so old as to be past all sympathetic feelings.

He was a mere mummy, this old man who had been celebrated as a teacher of singing in the days of Pasta and Malibran; a faint shadow of his former self, only kept alive by the mechanical exercise of his art. Yet, in spite of his great age, his ear was wonderfully keen and true; the sense of hearing, from continuous cultivation, being the only one which had survived the wreck of his faculties, and with the assistance of Bianca, he was still enabled to teach his wonderful system in an intelligible manner. Many of his pupils had been European, celebrities on the operatic stage during the past fifty years, and his rooms in Milan were crowded with souvenirs of famous artists of undying fame. His children, and, with the exception of Bianca, his grandchildren, were all dead; his friends and acquaintances and the generation that knew him had all passed away; but this Nestor of lyrical art still survived, alone and sad, amid the ruins of his past. White-haired, wrinkled, blear-eyed, silent, he sat daily in his great armchair, taking but little notice of the life around him, save to ask childish questions or talk about some dead-and-gone singer whose fame had once filled the world; but place a baton in his hand, strike the piano, lift the voice, and this apparent corpse awoke to life. He beat time, he corrected the least false note, he explained the necessary instructions in a faltering voice, and, during the lesson, bore at least some semblance of life; but when all was finished, the baton fell from his withered hand as he relapsed into his former apathy. One would have thought that he would have been glad to rest in his old age, but such was his love for his art that he insisted upon teaching still, and it was this alone which kept him alive. His granddaughter, Bianca, trained in the family traditions, was enabled to interpret his words, and, as his system of singing was unique, in spite of his apparent uselessness, he had many pupils.

Bianca herself was a charming Italian girl of twenty, more like a graceful white lily in appearance than anything else, so fragile, so delicate, so pallid did she seem. Her mournful eyes, dark and soft as those of a gazelle, seemed too large for her pale, oval face; and her figure, small and slender, always put me in mind of that of a fairy. Indeed, in sport, I sometimes called her the Fairy of Midnight, after some poet-fancy that haunted my brain, for all her strength seemed to have gone into those glorious masses of raven-black hair, coiled so smoothly round her small head. This portraiture seems to give the idea that Bianca was a melancholy young person, yet such was not the case, for I have seen her as gay as a bird on bright days, or when she received a letter from her lover.

Yes! she had a lover to whom she was engaged to be married, but, curiously enough, I knew nothing about this lover, not being intimate enough with Bianca to be the confidant of her tender little secret. This unknown lover was always away in other parts of Italy, and when he did visit Bianca it was during my absence, so I used to joke with the Signorina about this visionary being. But she, with one delicate finger on her lip and an arch smile of glee, would tell me that he—she never mentioned his name—that he had an actual existence, and some day I would see him in person at Verona. Well, here was Verona, here was Bianca, but the lover had not appeared, so I would have jestingly asked this Fairy of Midnight the reasons of his absence, had not the real grief expressed on her face deterred me.

"Signorina, are you in trouble?"

"Yes, yes! Signore, great trouble; but you cannot help me. No one can help me."

"But perhaps I——"

"No, Signore, it is useless. Come, you must have the lesson at once. The Maestro is dull to-day, he needs amusement; so come, the lesson."

"It is very cruel of you to make a joke of my lesson, Signorina."

Bianca made no reply to my jesting remark, but heaving a little sigh, placed the ivory baton in the hand of the Maestro and sat down at the piano. The mummy, finding his services required, woke up and had a little conversation with me before beginning the lesson.

"Eh! Signor Inglése," he croaked—this being his name for me—"London is dark!"

He had a fearful prejudice against London, which he had once visited at a foggy season, and always made the above remark to his English pupils, which no one ever thought of contradicting.

"Yes, yes!" he said, nodding his old head like a Chinese mandarin; "London is always dark."

"Yes, Maestro."

"You've not been working?"

"Indeed I have, Maestro."

"Come then, Signor Inglése, we will see," and the lesson commenced.

Oh, those lessons! what agonies I suffered during them, trying to attain the impossible! To how many fits of despair have I given way in failing time after time to manage my breathing! It was all breathing—a deep drawing in, a slow letting out—the exercise of internal muscles of which I had never heard even the name—the weariness of incessantly practising notes in a still, small voice hardly audible,—it was enough to discourage the most persevering. Some of the female pupils, I believe, cried with vexation when not able to do what was required by the severe Maestro, who denied the existence of the word "impossible" in connection with singing; but I, not being a woman, was reduced to swearing, which certainly relieved my feelings after a battle with a particularly aggravating exercise.

Even now, when I am successful in my art, I often turn cold as I think of those apparently insurmountable obstacles which I had to overcome; but with these painful memories there is mixed at the same time a kindly thought of that noble old Maestro, so patient, so courteous, so painstaking, whose devotion to his art was so great, who was so severe on the least fault and so encouraging of the least success in conquering a difficulty.

Well, the lesson went on slowly with frequent interruptions from the Maestro, who was satisfied with nothing less than perfection, and I breathed according to directions, sang "ah!" "eh," "ee's" in a tiny, tiny voice, until at the end of the hour I was glad to sit down and rest before departing. I felt tired out, I felt hungry, and, as the weather was bad, I felt cross, but at the same time I felt curious to know what was the matter with Bianca.

The Maestro, having remarked encouragingly that I had the voice of a goose and would never sing in La Scala, relapsed into silence, evidently thinking of his colezione which was being prepared in the kitchen with some trouble, judging from the raised, tones of Petronella's voice; and as Bianca still sat at the piano, striking random chords, there was nothing for me to do but to take my departure. She was not prepared to tell me her trouble, and indeed she had no reason to do so, but feeling anxious to aid the poor child if I could, I ventured to speak to her on the subject.

***

CHAPTER V

LOST

While I was wondering which was the best way to approach this somewhat delicate matter, the door was flung open to its fullest extent and Petronella stalked majestically into the room. There was a wrathful look on her strongly marked features, and Bianca trembled in expectation of a storm. Both she and the Maestro were terribly afraid of Petronella, who ruled the household and looked after them as she would a couple of children, so now that she frowned they acted like children; and were cowed by her eagle eye. Petronella surveyed the three of us grimly, and, being satisfied that her entrance had produced an effect, spoke with a dramatic gesture that Rachel herself might have envied,—

"I am enraged to-day. Let no one speak to me." Neither the Maestro nor Bianca seemed inclined to accept this tread-on-the-tail-of-my-coat challenge, so Petronella looked from one to the other to see on whom she should pour out the vials of her wrath. Ultimately she chose Bianca.

"Ah, it is you, Signorina! it is you who enrage me. And for why? you ask. Holy Saints! you ask why. Because you sit there like a statue in the Duoma. Will that bring him back? say I. No, Signora, let the bad young man go. Ecco!"

"Guiseppe is not a bad young man," cried Bianca, rising angrily to her feet.

"Are you older than I am, piccola? No! Have you been married like I was? No! Then let me speak, child that you are. All men are bad—ask the Signor there! All men are bad!"

Petronella made a comprehensive sweep of her arms so as to indicate the whole masculine portion of the human race, and I, seeing an opportunity of finding out what was the matter, did not attempt to defend masculine depravity in any way, but artfully asked a question,—

"I can hardly say. I don't know what you are talking about!"

"Eh! has the Signore no ears? I speak of Guiseppe Pallanza!"

"What, the tenor at the Teatro Ezzelino?"

"Yes, Signore, he is the engaged one of the Signorina here, and——"

"Enough, enough, Petronella!" cried Bianca, her face flushing. "Do not trouble the Signor with these chatterings."

"Oh, it's no trouble," I replied quickly. "Perhaps I can help you, Signorina, if you require help!"

"Eh, eh!" assented Petronella approvingly, "the English have long heads, piccola. Tell him all and he will find out what others cannot find out. And you, Maestro, the colezione is ready."

She tenderly led the old man into the next room, and I was thus left alone with Bianca, who had retreated to the window, where she stood twisting her handkerchief with nervous confusion.

"Do not tell me, Signorina, if you would rather not," I said gently.

"Ah, Signore, if I thought you would be my friend!"

"Certainly I will be your friend."

"The Maestro is so old. Petronella is so foolish. We know none in Verona, and I can do nothing for my poor Guiseppe!"

"Your lover, Signorina?"

"Yes. I promised you should see him at Verona, but—now—ah now!—but perhaps you have heard him singing at the Ezzelino?"

"No; I have not been to the opera since my arrival here. What is the matter with him? Is he ill?"

"I know not! I know not! He is lost!"

"Lost?"

"Yes, Signore. My Guiseppe has disappeared and no one knows where he is!"

Could there be any connection between the disappearance of Guiseppe and the death of that young man I had seen in the fatal chamber? The thought flashed across me as she spoke, but I dismissed it as idle.

"And you want some one to look for Signor Pallanza?"

"Yes, yes!"

"Well, I will undertake the task."

"You, Signore!" she cried joyfully; "will you search for him?"

"Certainly, Signorina; I promised to be your friend. Now sit down, and tell me all about your lover and his disappearance. I may be able to do more for you than you think."

The fact is, that by some subtle instinct I connected the disappearance of this young man with the curious events of two nights before, and, leading Bianca to a seat, I prepared to listen attentively to her recital.

"Signore," she began in her flute-like voice, "I have been engaged to marry Guiseppe Pallanza for some months. He was a pupil of the Maestro, and we loved each other when we first met; but ah! Signore, he was poor then, and we could not marry, but now he is rich and famous."

"Yes, I have heard of the tenor Pallanza, but have never seen him on the stage."

"He has the voice of a god, Signore, and at La Scala, two seasons ago—oh, Signore, it was the talk of the whole city. The papers called him the New Mario, and he is so handsome—like an angel. After La Scala he went to Florence, to Naples, and then to Rome, where he sang in 'Faust' and 'Polyeuct' at the Apollo, then he came on here a week ago for the season at the Ezzelino; but now he is lost. Dio! how unhappy I am."

She covered her face with her hands, and wept quietly for a few minutes, and, impatient as I was to hear the particulars of the affair, I did not dare to disturb her grief. After a time she dried her tears, and went on again,—

"He came to Verona on Saturday, Signore, and we were so happy together talking about our marriage; and on Monday he sang in 'Faust' at the Ezzelino. I went to the theatre with Petronella, and that was the last time I saw him."

"Oh, then he disappeared on Monday night!" I asked quickly, feeling my heart begin to beat rapidly with excitement, for it was on Monday night that my extraordinary adventure had taken place.

"Yes, Signore. He was to come here after the opera, to tell the Maestro how he had sung—you know how anxious the Maestro is over his pupils, but he never came, nor the next day either; so this morning I went to ask at the Ezzelino, and they told me he had disappeared."

"It's curious I never heard of it. The disappearance of a popular tenor is not a common thing!"

"Signore, he sang on Monday and was to sing again to-night, so nothing was thought about him not coming to the theatre yesterday; but this morning they sent to his lodgings, to find that he had not been there since he left the Ezzelino after the opera on Monday."

"The papers will be full of it to-night!"

"Ah! that will not bring him back," said poor little Bianca in a melancholy tone, shaking her small head, which drooped like a faded flower.

I was now certain that my adventure on Monday night had something to do with the disappearance of Guiseppe Pallanza, and doubtless the young man I had seen in the deserted palace was the missing tenor; but the antique dress, the amorous rendezvous—these needed some explanation.

"Was he in love with any one, Signorina?"

It was a cruel but necessary question which angered Bianca, who threw back her little head with great haughtiness.

"Signore, he loved me and no one else."

A Creature of the Night

"Had he any reason for disappearing?"

"Signore!"

"Forgive me if I appear rude," I said in a deprecating tone; "but indeed, Signorina, to find out all I must know all."

"Well, Signore, I am telling you all," she replied petulantly. "It was most strange his going away from the theatre."

"How so?"

"He left the Ezzelino in his stage-dress!"

"Ah!"

I jumped to my feet in a state of uncontrollable excitement, for I saw at once that I was on the right track. The antique dress was explained now! it was the dress he wore in the last act of "Faust."

"But surely, Signorina, that was very extraordinary," I said, pausing in my walk; "no one would walk the streets of Verona in a dress like that."

"I can explain that, Signore. When Guiseppe came from Rome, a friend came with him who was very ill—a baritone singer, who was in the same company at the Apollo. I was told at the Ezzelino that just before the last act of the opera, Guiseppe received a note saying that his friend was dying, so as soon as the curtain fell, he threw on a cloak which hid his dress, and went away as quickly as possible, so as to see his friend before he died."

"Oh! and is the friend dead yet?"

"I do not know, Signore."

The story of the dying friend might be true, yet to me it seemed highly improbable, and I guessed that the people at the theatre had told this fiction to pacify the fears of Signorina Angello, to whom they knew that Pallanza was engaged. The real truth of the matter was doubtless that the letter came from the woman I had followed, asking him to meet her at the deserted Palazzo Morone, and he had gone there innocently enough to be poisoned as I had seen. This explained a great deal, but it did not explain why the meeting should have taken place at such an extraordinary spot, and why the woman should have come from a burial-ground to keep the appointment. Taking all the circumstances into consideration, I was certain that it was Pallanza I had seen murdered on Monday night, but in order to be quite sure of his identity, I asked Bianca if she had any photograph of her betrothed.

"Of a surety, Signore," she replied, and going to an album on the table, brought me a cabinet portrait. "This is Guiseppe as Faust, the dress in which he left the theatre."

It was as I surmised. The portrait was coloured, and I saw an exact representation of the young man I had beheld at the Palazzo Morone. The typical Italian face with the black curly hair, dark eyes, small moustache and sallow skin; the slender figure arrayed in a doublet of blue velvet, slashed with white satin; the azure silk cloak, the poniard and the high riding-boots—nothing was wanting; the successful tenor of the portrait was the man who had taken poison from the hand of the lady of the sepulchre. Still it was no use telling Bianca of my suspicions until I had discovered the whole secret; and besides, as Guiseppe was dead, I naturally shrank from being the bearer of such bad news. I suppose my face betrayed my thoughts, for I saw the Signorina watching me anxiously; so to lull any fancies she might have, I made the first remark that came into my head,—

"I never saw Faust in riding-boots before!"

"Ah, Signore!" replied the girl with a fond look, "Guiseppe was an artist as well as a singer, and designed his own dresses. He said that as Faust in the last act was going to fly with Marguerite, and Mephistopheles speaks of the horses waiting, it is natural that he should wear a riding-dress."

This explanation was quite satisfactory, and having thus learned the identity of the young man whom I had seen murdered, I prepared to go, when another idea entered my head, and, going over to the piano, I began to play by ear the strange air I had heard at the Palazzo Morone. Bianca gave a cry of surprise as she heard the melody, and came over to the piano with a puzzled look on her face.

"Ah, you know it, Signorina?" I said, turning round quickly.

"Yes! in fact I gave it to Guiseppe. It is an old air by Palestrina, which I found among the music of the Maestro, to which Guiseppe set words. He is very fond of it and sings it a great deal. Ah, Signore, you must have heard him sing it, for no one else has a copy."

I turned off the matter with a careless remark, not caring to tell Bianca where I had heard it; and now being quite certain that I would be able to unravel the whole mystery, I wanted to get away as quickly as possible in order to arrange my plans.

"Addio, Signorina," I said, giving her my hand. "When I see you again I may be able to give you news."

"Good news?"

"Yes, I hope so, Signorina," I replied hurriedly as Petronella appeared at the door. "Do not anticipate evil, I beg of you. I have no doubt Guiseppe is quite well."

"Oh, I hope so! I trust so! Addio! Signor Hugo, you will come back soon?"

"To-morrow, Signorina."

"Ah! I see you have brought back the smiles," said Petronella's gruff voice as she ushered me out. "What do you think of this evil one going away, Signore? I was going to have four masses if he is dead, but those priests are such thieves. Ecco!"

"Why should you think he is dead, Petronella?"

"Eh, Signore, he loves the piccola so much that nothing but death would keep him away."

"Except—"

"I know what you would say, Signore, except a woman. Well, maybe men are all bad. I've been married, Signore—I know, I know."

"Well, I don't think I'm particularly bad, Petronella."

"Eh! then you're not a true man, Signore," retorted Petronella, closing the argument and the door at the same time.

***

CHAPTER VI

A HAUNTED PALACE

I need hardly say that I was very much excited over the strange discovery I had made, as there now appeared to be a reasonable chance of clearing up the mystery of the Palazzo Morone. I had discovered the name of the unhappy young man, which gave me a most important clue to the reading of the enigma; but I had yet to find out the name of the lady who had behaved in such an extraordinary manner and committed so daring a crime. After hearing Peppino's story I fancied that she might perchance be the Contessa Morone, but had later on dismissed this idea as idle, seeing that she had been absent from Verona for many months; but now that Bianca had told me that Pallanza had come straight from Rome, I began to suspect that I had been right in my surmise. According to Peppino the Contessa had taken up her residence at the Italian capital, so what was more likely than that she had fallen in love with Guiseppe while he was singing at the Teatro Apollo, and, following him to Verona, had killed him by means of poison, in revenge for his determination to leave her?

So far everything was feasible enough, but two points of the affair perplexed me very much, one being the choosing of the deserted palace as a place of meeting, the other the visit to the burial ground by the woman. We do not live in the times of the Borgias, when noble ladies can thus rid themselves of their lovers with impunity, else I might have believed that this phantom of Donna Lucrezia had gone to the old Veronese cemetery to select a grave for the unfortunate young man she intended to murder. To think thus, however, was foolish, and although I guessed that she had used the old palace of her family as a safe place for a lovers' meeting, seeing its gruesome reputation secured it from public curiosity, yet I was quite unable to explain the cemetery mystery. One thing, however, appeared to me to be certain, that Guiseppe Pallanza had been carrying on an intrigue with the Contessa—presuming the ghoul to be her—and that he had gone to the Palazzo Morone on the night in question at her request. As to the sick friend——

Now I greatly mistrusted that sick-friend story. So many fast young Englishmen whom I knew had adopted the same lie to cover their little peccadilloes that I was quite sure Pallanza had employed the same fiction to prevent the scandal of his intrigue with this unknown woman from reaching the ears of his **fiancée**. Bianca was a very proud girl, and I felt certain, from what little I had seen of her character, that if she discovered Guiseppe was playing her false, she would at once break off the engagement at any cost. Like all Italian women, when she loved she loved with her whole soul, and expected the same single-hearted return to her passion; so that the discovery of her lover's infidelity could only be punished sufficiently, according to her ideas, by an everlasting parting between them. Pallanza knew this, and therefore tried to hide his guilt by the plausible story of his dying friend, which appeared to me to be such a remarkably weak fabrication that, before going to the Palazzo Morone, I determined to find out if this mythical invalid existed.

Curiously enough, although I was studying for the musical profession and was devoted to operatic performances, I had not been to the Teatro Ezzelino since my arrival at Verona, preferring to wander about the streets of the romantic old city in the moonlight to sitting night after night in a stifling atmosphere of heat, glare, and noise. I made up my mind, however, to go on this special night, in the hope that I might hear some talk about Pallanza's disappearance, and be guided thereby in any future movements; but meantime I went to the theatre in the afternoon, and, introducing myself to the impresario as a friend of Guiseppe's, asked him if he had heard any news of the missing tenor.

The impresario, a dingy old man of doubtful cleanliness, was in despair, and raged against the absent Pallanza like a Garrick of the gutter. He had heard nothing of this birbánte—this ladrone who had thus disappeared, and left an honest impresario in the lurch. "Faust" was the success of the season; without Pallanza there could be no "Faust," and the season would be a failure. What was he to do? Cospetto! it was the luck of the devil. Why had this scellerato run away? A sick friend? Bah! there was no sick friend. It was a woman who had enticed away this pazzo. A dying friend from Rome was not a very likely story, but a lie—a large and magnificent lie. Here was the basso of his company, who had been singing with Pallanza at the Apollo; ask him, truth is on his lips, Behold this good man!

Signor Basso-profundo advanced, and though truth might have been on his lips it certainly was not apparent on his face, for a more deceitful countenance I never beheld. However, I have no doubt he spoke truth on this occasion, as there was no money to be made by telling a lie, and he confirmed the words of the wrathful impresario. The sick friend was a myth, but in Rome Pallanza had been friendly with a lady. Per Bacco! a great lady, but the name was unknown to him. It appeared that Signor Basso-profundo dressed in the same room as Pallanza, and it was just before the last act of "Faust" that Guiseppe received the note. He told the basso-profundo that it was from a dying friend, and had departed quickly when the opera was ended, in his stage-dress, with a cloak wrapped round him. The basso-profundo was sure the note was from a lady. The impresario was also sure, and devoted the lady in question to the infernal gods with a richness of expression I have never heard equalled in any language.

Having thus found out what I suspected from the first, that the dying friend was a mere invention to cloak an intrigue, I left the impresario to tear his hair and call Guiseppe names in company with Signor Basso-profundo, and went back to my hotel, where I found Peppino waiting with his fiacre to drive me to the Palazzo Morone.

He was still unwilling to take me to this place of evil reputation, and made one last effort to shake my determination by gruesome stories of

A Creature of the Night

people who had gone into the palazzo and never came out again; but I laughed at all these hobgoblin romances, and getting into the fiacre, told him to drive off at once, which he did, after crossing himself twice, so as to secure his own safety should the ghosts of Palazzo Morone take a fancy to carry me off as a heretic.

We speedily left the broad, modern streets, and rattled down gloomy, mediæval passages, the humid atmosphere of which chilled me to the bone, in spite of the heat of the day. The fiacre—with its jingling bells—bumped on the uneven stones, turned abruptly round unexpected corners, corkscrewed itself between narrow walls, crept under low archways, and after innumerable dodgings, twistings, hairbreadth escapes from upsettings, and perilous balancings on the edges of drains, at length emerged into that queer little piazza at the end of which I saw the great façade of the richly-decorated palace I had beheld in the moonlight of two nights before.

I had been an ardent student of Baedeker since my arrival in Italy, and from the fortified appearance of the palazzo, judged that it had been built by Michelo Sammicheli, who, according to the guide-book, was the greatest military architect of the middle ages. The building was four stories high, with long lines of narrow windows closely barred by curiously ornamented iron cages—which bulged outward,——as a protection against thieves or enemies, and the whole front was adorned with almost obliterated paintings after the style of the Genoese palaces. In addition to the brush, the chisel had done its work, and wreaths of flowers, grinning masks, nude figures of boys and girls, elaborate crests and armorial devices with fishes, birds, tritons, shells, and fruit were sculptured round the windows, along the fortified castellated top, and over the great portal. All the square in front of this splendid specimen of Renaissance art was overgrown with grass. The houses on every side were also deserted, and what with the broken windows, the empty piazza, and the closed doors, everything had a melancholy, desolate appearance, as if a curse rested upon the whole neighbourhood.

Peppino evidently was of this opinion, for although it was broad daylight, and the hot sunlight poured down on the grass-grown square, yet he kept muttering prayers in a low voice; and if by chance he looked towards the Palazza, he always crossed himself with great devoutness. I was not, however, going to be baulked of my intention by any superstitious feeling on the part of an Italian cab-driver, so I ordered Peppino to tie up his horse and come with me into the palace. This modest request, however, so horrified Peppino that he absolutely squeaked with horror, like a rabbit caught in a snare.

"I, Signore!" he whimpered, touching the relic on his breast. "Dio! not to be King of Italy would I go into that house! If you are wise, Signore, look and come away lest evil befall you. Cospetto! Signore, remember the Frate. Think of Madonna Matilda!"

"What about Madonna Matilda, Peppino?"

"Eh, Illustrious, do you not know? She was a friend of his Holiness at Canossa, and, though a woman, wanted to celebrate mass, but Il Cristo burnt her to ashes with fire from above!—and she died. Ecco! Cospetto! Signore, it is foolish to meddle with holy things."

"Well, you can't call this palace holy, Peppino?"

"No, Illustrious. It is accursed!" replied the Italian, crossing himself, "but there is fire below as well as above, and you are a heretic."

"Which means that I had better beware of the devil! eh, Peppino. Well, well; I'm not afraid, so I will enter the palace, and if you see me carried off by the ghosts, you can tell the carabinieri."

"Dio! Illustrious, do not jest; but if you will go you must go. I will wait here and pray for your soul."

Peppino was as obstinate as a mule in his fear of ghosts, so leaving him to smoke his long Italian cigar and watch the brown lizards scuttling over the hot stones in the sunshine, I advanced towards the palace with the determination to find out the secret chamber. As I knew it would be dark therein, owing to its want of windows, I had taken the precaution to provide myself with a candle and a box of matches. Feeling that these were safe in my pocket, I went to the iron gate and entered the courtyard in the same way as I had done on that night. This time, however, I examined the ironwork, and found to my surprise that the missing bar had been half filed through and then wrenched away. The marks left were quite fresh, and it had been done so recently that the bar had not had time to grow rusty. This discovery astonished me not a little, as I did not see the reason of such an entrance being made. If it were the Contessa who used the palace, she would have the key of the side door, and could thus admit herself and her lover at her pleasure, while this breach could only have been made by some one who could not enter in any other way.

I thought of the person into whose arms I had fallen, the person who had placed a handkerchief wet with some liquid over my face, and although, according to Peppino's story, this watcher at the door was the phantom of Count Mastino Morone, yet dismissing such an explanation as due to superstition, I began to think that another person had followed the lady of the sepulchre besides myself. Yes, there could be no doubt about it, some third person had tracked her to the palazzo, and, unable to enter in the ordinary way, had filed through and broken the iron bar in the gate. Gaining access to the interior of the palazzo in this way, the unknown had penetrated to the secret chamber, and doubtless had witnessed the same strange scene as I had done. My presence had been discovered, and to preserve for some unknown reason, the secret of this terrible chamber, I had been seized, rendered insensible by chloroform, and taken to the Piazza Vittorio Emanuele, so that I would be unable to re-discover the Palazzo Morone.

All these thoughts flashed through my brain with the rapidity of lightning, and I wondered whom this unknown could be—a friend of Pallanza? an accomplice of the Contessa! I did not know what to think, so leaving all such conjectures to a more seasonable time, I crossed over the dreary courtyard and entered the great hall.

It was a magnificent entrance, and when thronged with courtiers, men-at-arms, pages, and ladies, must have presented a noble appearance. Of enormous size, the high walls and lofty roof were painted with glowing frescoes representing the ancient glories of the Republic, and the floor was brilliant with gorgeous mosaics of coats-of-arms and fantastic figures. The painted windows on either side of the huge portal blazed with variegated tints, and the bright sun streaming in through the glass—as many-coloured as Joseph's coat—dyed the floor with vivid lights and gaudy hues. Ancient tapestries hung here and there between the two lines of black marble columns running down the sides of the hall, and the wind, stealing in through the open door, shook the grey dust from these mouldering splendours of the loom. At the end of this immense vestibule arose a broad staircase of white marble with balustrades of elaborate bronze fretwork, and from the first landing two other flights sloped off to right and left of the main branch. All the air was filled with floating shadows, the soft wind moved the hangings without sound, and I was alone in the deserted hall, over which brooded an intense silence, which made me shiver in the chill atmosphere pervading this abode of desolation.

However, the afternoon was passing quickly, and as I had plenty to do before nightfall, I rapidly ascended the shallow stairs. Turning to the right, which was the way the unknown lady had taken the other night, I soon found myself in the long corridor with the windows looking out on to the courtyard. Many of these were broken, but others were quite whole, their colours as bright and glowing as when they had first been placed there.

At the end of the corridor I turned to the left, and found the short flight of shallow steps, which, however, led up into darkness, so that before ascending them I had to light my candle. Luckily there were no draughts, for the air was absolutely still, and the flame of my candle burned clear and steadily. Up these steps I went, entered the short corridor, and paused before the heavy door which gave admission into the ante-chamber of the fatal room. Realizing what had taken place inside on that fatal night, I dreaded to enter, lest I should find the corpse of the unfortunate Pallanza on the floor; but overcoming my emotions, with a strong effort I thrust open the door and entered.

The tapestried chamber presented exactly the same appearance, with the small table in the centre, the burnt-out torch lying on the floor, and at the end the rich folds of the gold-worked curtains veiling the entrance to the inner apartment. I stood on the threshold, half expecting to hear the shrill notes of the mandolin, and the passionate song ring through the silence, but all was still and mute, as if it were indeed the tomb of the dead I expected to find.

At last, with a thrill of dread, I parted the heavy curtains and found myself in the circular chamber. The faint light of the candle just hollowed out a gulf in the Cimmerian darkness, and I saw the dim glitter of the gold and silver on the table, the ghastly glimmer of the white cloth, and the sparks of weak fire flashing from the tarnished gold embroidery of the curtains. All was as I had seen it—the eight white pillars, the dull-red hangings with their Arabesque patterns of golden thread, the gilt table, the massive metal goblets and silver candelabra, even the half-eaten fruit, with everything on the table in disorder; but, somewhat to my relief, I found nothing else. The dead body, which I had seen lying at the feet of that terrible woman, had vanished, and although I searched over every inch of the chamber, I could find no trace of the fearful crime which had been committed. The demon who had enticed the unhappy young man to his ruin had completed her evil work by secreting his body, and I began to think that all trace of Guiseppe Pallanza had disappeared from the earth for evermore.

Who was this woman who, in this room, had so wickedly slain her lover? Who was the man—I felt sure it was a man—who had seized me at the door, and borne me insensible from the palace? I could answer neither of these questions, and had it not been for the story of Bianca, for the disappearance of Pallanza, I would have fancied the whole some hideous dream, some nightmare of medieval devilry, which had filled my brain with the phantasmagoria of delirium. Everything, however, was too real, too terrible, to admit of such an explanation; so as I could discover nothing more from examining the chamber I prepared to leave. The atmosphere yet had a faint aroma of the sandalwood perfume which emanated from the unknown woman; at my feet still lay the broken mandolin; and the rich wine-cups still glittered in the dim light. I no longer wondered at such wealth being left here undefended, for superstition, more of a safeguard than bolts and bars, protected this cave of Aladdin from thievish Italian fingers;

and even if a thief had known of these riches, I doubt whether he would have had the courage to dare the unseen horrors of the palazzo.

For myself, standing there in the perfumed atmosphere, with the light just showing the intense gloom, the dim glitter of gold and silver, the absolute stillness and the horrible memories of the chamber—I felt as though I were in the presence of the dead. At the table sat the phantoms of Donna Renata and her lover, smiling at one another with hatred in their ghostly hearts; at the door watched the evil face of the outraged husband awaiting the consummation of the tragedy; and in imagination I could see the wicked smile of the woman, the scowl of the husband, the loathing look on the face of the lover. My breath, coming quick and fast, made the flame of the candle flicker and flare until, overcome by the horror of the room, and by the workings of my imagination, I turned and fled—fled from the evil gloom, from that blood-stained splendour, out into the blessed sunshine and pure air of heaven.

"Dio!" cried Peppino, as I walked quickly out into the square, "how pale you are, Illustrious! Eh, Signore, have the ghosts——"

"I have seen no ghosts, Peppino, but I have felt their presence."

"Cospetto! did I not warn the Signore against the accursed place? Come, Illustrious, jump in and we will leave this abode of devils."

"Very well, Peppino," I replied, entering the fiacre, "but drive slowly, as I want to know the way to this palazzo."

"Dio! the Signore will not come again?"

"Yes! I am coming some night this month."

"Saints! the Signore is mad and lost!" muttered Peppino with a pale face. Then, hastily gathering up the reins, he drove rapidly away from the lonely square, leaving this gruesome palace to the night and to the feast of ghosts.

***

CHAPTER VII

AT THE TEATRO EZZELINO

From my mother I had inherited one of those highly strung organizations which are largely affected by their surroundings, and which, like an Æolian harp, to the sighing wind vibrate with every breath of passion that passes over them—organizations which take their colour, their bias, their desires from the last event which occurs, and which are entirely in sympathy with the predominating feeling of the moment. In childhood this dangerous spirit of moods and fancies had been fostered by an old Scottish nurse, who used to thrill me with wild stories of Highland superstitions, and with weird ballads of elfish fantasy; but since I had mixed in the world I had learned to control and sway my imaginative faculty, and had thus acquired a command over myself. But, as I said before, superstition is in every one, and waxes or wanes according to their surroundings; so the terrors of childish tales, which had been half-forgotten in the bustle of worldly life, now came upon my soul with full force in this haunted city of Verona. The burial-ground, the ghostly room, the accursed palace, the phantoms of evil-seeming, all these peopled the chambers of my brain, with their unreal horrors, until I became so nervous and unstrung, that every sudden noise, every unexpected sound, and every shadowy comer, made me thrill with supernatural fear as if I were again a child listening to tales of devildom.

I knew this mood was a bad one, and would have sought cheerful society to drive away the evil spirit had I known where to seek it. But there were no English at my hotel, and, in the present state of affairs, the Casa Angello was not particularly cheerful, so as I did not care about spending a lonely evening, I methought myself of my intention to go to the Teatro Ezzelino. On glancing at the paper I saw that the opera for the night was "Lucrezia Borgia;" and this name gave me a renewed sensation of horror. The lady of the sepulchre had taken in my imagination the semblance of Ferrara's Duchess, and the memory of the terrible daughter of Pope Alexander seemed never to leave me. She had come from the graveyard, she had supped in the fatal chamber, she had murdered her lover; and now, when she had vanished into thin air, I was to see her represented on the stage in all her magnificent wickedness. I had a good mind not to go, but seeing that there was a ballet after the opera, I thought I would brave this phantom of the brain, and find in the lightness of the dancing an antidote to the gloomy terrors of the lyrical drama.

The cooking at my hotel was somewhat better than the usual run of Italian culinary ideas, so I made an excellent dinner, drank some Asti Spumati, an agreeable wine of an exhilarating nature, and felt much better when I started for the Ezzelino.

It was one of those perfect Italian evenings such as one sees depicted by the glowing brush of Turner, and there yet lingered in the quiet evening sky a faint purple reflection of the sunset glories. No moon as yet, but here and there a burning star throbbing in the deep heart of the sky, and under the peaceful heavens the weather-worn red roofs and grey walls of antique Verona mellowed to warm loveliness in the twilight shadows. Beautiful as it was, however, with the memory of that eerie night still on me, I had no desire to renew my moonlight wanderings, so, without pausing to admire the enchanting scene, I hastened on to the theatre to be in time for the first notes of Donnizetti's opera.

The Teatro Ezzelino is a very charming opera-house, built in a light, airy fashion, with plenty of ventilation, a thing to be grateful for on hot summer nights. All the decorations are white and gold, so that it has a delightfully cool appearance; nevertheless, what with the warmth of the season without, and the glaring heat of the gas within, I felt unpleasantly hot. The gallery and stalls were crowded, but as it was only eight o'clock, most of the boxes were empty, and I knew would not be filled until late in the evening by those who, tired of the well-known music of "Lucrezia," wanted to see the new ballet.

Having glanced round the theatre, I bought a book of the words, hired an opera-glass from an obsequious attendant, and settled myself comfortably for the evening. The orchestra—a very excellent one, directed by Maestro Feraldi, of Milan—played the prelude in a sufficiently good style, and the pictured curtain arose on the well-known Venetian scene which I had so often beheld. The chorus, in their heterogeneous costumes of no known age, wandered about in their usual aimless fashion, shouted their approval of smiling Venice in the ordinary indifferent style; and a very good contralto who sang Orsini, having delivered her first aria with great dramatic fervour, they all vanished from the stage, leaving the sleeping Genaro to be contemplated by Lucrezia Borgia.

I was disappointed with the Duchess when she arrived, and I must say that my majestic evil lady of the sepulchre looked far more like the regal sister of Cæsar Borgia than this diminutive singer with the big voice, who raged round the stage like a spitfire, and gave one no idea of the terrible Medusa of Ferrara, whose smile was death to all, lovers and friends alike. The tenor was a long individual, and Lucrezia being so small, their duets, in point of physical appearance, were sufficiently ridiculous; but as they sang well together, their rendering of the characters, artistically speaking, was enjoyable. The chorus entered and discovered Lucrezia with Genaro; the prima-donna defied them all with the look and ways of a cross child; there was the usual dramatic chorus, and the curtain fell on the prologue with but slight applause. I did not go out, as I felt very comfortable, so amused myself with looking round the house, when, during the first act of the opera, two officers entered the theatre and took their seats in front of mine; They were two gay young men, who talked a great deal about one thing and another in such raised voices that I could hear all they said, some of which was not particularly edifying.

During the first act which succeeds the prologue they were comparatively quiet, but when Lucrezia entered in the second to sing the celebrated duet with Alfonso, they were loud in their expressions of disapproval concerning her appearance. The music of this part of the opera is particularly loud and noisy, but even through the crash of the orchestra I could hear their expressions of disapproval.

"The voice is not bad, but the appearance—the acting—oime!"

"Eh, Teodoro, what would you? Donna Lucrezia is not on the stage."

"Not on the stage!" said Teodoro in an astonished tone. "Ebbene! where is she?"

"Look at the box yonder!"

"Per Bacco! the Contessa Morone."

I started as I heard this name, and, looking in the same direction as the young men, saw a woman seated far back in the shadow of a box, the fourth or fifth from the stage. She was talking to three gentlemen, and her face was turned away so that I could not see her features; but, judging from the glimpse I caught of her head and bust, she seemed to be a very majestic woman.

The Contessa Morone! She was then in Verona after all. This discovery removed all my doubts concerning the identity of the ghoul. She was the woman who had left the vault in the burial-ground. She was the woman who had slain Guiseppe Pallanza in the secret chamber of the deserted palace, and she was the woman seated in the shadow of the box, talking idly as though she had no terrible crime to burden her conscience. If I could only see her face I would then recognise her; but, as if she had some presentiment of danger, she persistently looked everywhere but in my direction. As I gazed she moved slightly, the bright light of a lamp shone on her neck, and I saw a sudden tongue of red flame flash through the semi-twilight of the box, which at once reminded me of the necklace of rubies worn by that terrible vampire of the graveyard.

Eager to know all about this woman, whom I felt sure was the murderess of Pallanza, I listened breathlessly to the two officers who were still talking about her.

"It is a year since Morone died," said Teodoro, lowering his opera-glass, "and she has lived since at Rome, where I met her. Why has she returned here?"

A Creature of the Night

"Eh, who knows! Perhaps to reside again at the Palazzo Morone."

"That tomb. Diamine! She must become a ghost to live there."

"Ebbene, Teodoro! the ghost of Lucrezia Borgia! Why does she not marry again?"

"Who knows! I wouldn't like to be her husband in spite of her money. Corpo di Bacco! a woman who sees in the dark like a cat."

"The evil eye!"

"Yes! and everything else that's wicked. I do not like that Signora at all."

"Che peccato! you might marry her."

"Or her money! Ecco!"

They both laughed, and, the act being ended, left their seats. I also went out into the corridor for a smoke and a breath of fresh air, feeling deeply sorry that this interesting conversation had been interrupted. From what one of the officers had said she was evidently a nyctalopyst, and could see in the dark, which accounted at once for the unerring way in which she had threaded the dark streets, and was also the reason that she now remained secluded in the shadow of her box, preferring the darkness to the light. Puzzling over these things, and wondering how I could get a glimpse of her face, I lighted a cigarette and strolled about in the vestibule of the theatre with the rest of the crowd.

There were a goodly number of civilians of all sizes, ages, and complexions, while the military element was represented by a fair sprinkling of officers in the picturesque uniforms of the Italian army. The air was thick with tobacco-smoke there was a clatter of vivacious voices, and the great doors of the theatre were thrown wide open to admit the fresh night air into the overpoweringly hot atmosphere. Being wrapt up in my ideas about the Contessa Morone and her extraordinary behaviour, I leaned against a pillar and took no notice of any one, when suddenly a tall officer stopped in front of me and held out his hand.

"What! Is it you, Signor Hugo? Come sta!"

"Beltrami! You here! I am surprised!"

"Ma foi," replied Beltrami, who constantly introduced French words into his conversation; "you are not so surprised as I am. I thought you were in your foggy island, and behold you appear at Verona. How did you come here? What are you doing? Eh! Hugo, tell me all."

I do not think I have mentioned Beltrami before, which is curious, considering I have been talking so much about Italy and the Italians; but the fact is, my friend the Marchese only now enters into this curious story I am relating, so thus being introduced in due season I will tell all I know about him.

During my narrative I fancy I have mentioned that I spoke and understood Italian tolerably for an Englishman. Well, I did not learn my Italian in Italy—no, indeed! Foggy London saw my maiden efforts to acquire that soft bastard Latin which Byron talks of, and the Marchese Luigi Beltrami gave me my first lessons in his melodious language. He had come to England some years before with a card of introduction to my father from a friend in Florence, and on being introduced to our household we had taken a great fancy to one another. Even in those days, perhaps as a premonitory symptom of my operatic leanings, I was mad on all things Italian, and discoursed about art, raved of Cimabue and Titian, and quoted Dante, Ariosto, and Alfieri until every one of my friends were, I am sure, heartily wearied of my enthusiasm. Beltrami appeared, and feeling flattered by my great admiration for his country, advised me to learn Italian. I did so, and with his help soon became no mean proficient in the tongue which the Marchese, being a Florentine, spoke very purely. In return I taught him English; but either I was a bad master, or Beltrami was an idle scholar, for all the English he ever learned consisted of two sentences: "You are a beautiful miss," and "I love you," but with these two he got along comparatively well, particularly with woman.

English ladies at first were indignant at this outspoken admiration, but Beltrami was so good-looking, and apparently so sincere in his use of these two English sentences, that they usually ended by pardoning him; nevertheless the Marchese found that if he wanted to get on in society he would have to moderate his transports. Ultimately, if I remember rightly, he took refuge in French, and said a great many pretty things in that very pretty tongue.

My friend Beltrami and myself were the antithesis of one another in character, as he had a great deal of the subtle craft of the old Italian despot about him; yet somehow we got on capitally together, perhaps by the law of contrast, and when he returned to Italy I was sorry to see the last of him. I promised to some day visit him at his palazzo in Florence, and fully intended to do so before leaving Italy; but here was Verona, and here, by the intervention of chance, was the Marchese, as suave, as subtle-faced, and as handsome as ever. He appeared to be delighted to see me, and as I was a stranger in a strange land, I was glad to find at least one familiar face.

In response to his request I told him about the death of my father, of my determination to study singing, and the circumstances which had led me to Verona, to all of which Beltrami listened attentively, and at the conclusion of my story shook hands with me again.

"Ebbene! my friend Hugo, I am glad to see you in our Italy. As you see, I serve the King and am stationed in his dismal palace, so while you are here I will make things pleasant. Ecco!"

"No, no! my dear Marchese, I know what you mean by making things pleasant. I have come here to work, not to play."

"Dame, mon ami! too much work is bad."

"Eh, Marchese, and too much play is worse; but tell me how have you been since I saw you last?"

"Oh, just the same; I am as poor as ever, but soon I will be rich!"

"Bravo, Beltrami! Is your uncle, the Cardinal, dead?"

"My uncle, the Cardinal, is immortal," replied the Marchese cynically. "No, he still lives in the hope to succeed to the Fisherman's Chair. I am going to be married!"

"I congratulate you."

"Eh, Hugo, I think you will when you see the future Marchesa! She is in the theatre to-night. I am engaged to marry her, and as she takes my friends for her own, come with me and I will introduce you."

I drew back, as I wanted to watch the Contessa Morone, and if I went to Beltrami's box I would perhaps lose sight of her.

"You must excuse me, Signor Luigi, because—because you see I am not in evening dress."

It was the best excuse I could think of, but, being a very weak one, Beltrami laughed, and, slipping his arm into mine, dragged me along the corridor.

"Sapristi! you talk like a child. You are my friend. Signora Morone will be delighted to see you. She adores the English."

"Madame Morone!" I exclaimed, thunderstruck.

"Yes, the Contessa! Do you know her by sight? Mon Dieu! is she not beautiful? You shall speak the English to her. She loves your foggy islanders."

I was so bewildered by the chance thrown in my way of finding out if the Contessa Morone had anything to do with the burial-ground episode, that I only replied to Beltrami's chatter by an uneasy laugh, and suffered myself to be led unresistingly along.

The Marchese did not take me into the box itself, but into one of those small ante-rooms, on the opposite side of the corridor, which are used by Italian ladies as reception saloons for their friends when at the theatre. I heard the loud chatter of many voices as Beltrami opened the door, and there, standing under the glare of the gas-lamp, with the wicked smile on her lips, the pearls in her hair, the ruby necklace round her throat, I saw the woman who had come from the vault, the woman who had poisoned Pallanza in the secret room, the phantom of Lucrezia Borgia.

***

CHAPTER VIII

THE PHANTOM OF LUCREZIA BORGIA

I was duly introduced by the Marchese, and Signora Morone received me in the most amiable manner. She was certainly a very charming woman, and had I not known her true character, I would doubtless have been fascinated by her gracious affability; but, in spite of her courtesy, I could hardly speak to her without a feeling of repulsion. This beautiful woman, so suave, so smiling, so seductive, inspired me with that sensation of absolute dread which one experiences at the sight of a sleek, velvet-footed pantheress—a comely beast to admire, but a terrible one to caress. I replied to her polite inquiries in a somewhat mechanical fashion, which she doubtless put down to my imperfect knowledge of Italian, for in spite of all my efforts to feel at ease in her society, yet I was unable to do more than behave with strained courtesy towards this woman whose mask I had torn off, whose secret I had penetrated, and the wickedness of whose heart I knew.

There were several other gentlemen in the room, who talked gaily with the Contessa, and amused themselves by eating the bonbons and crystallised fruits provided for refreshments. The last act of the opera had not yet commenced, so Signora Morone sank gracefully into a velvet-cushioned chair, and permitted her courtiers to retail all the news of the day for her amusement. I am afraid this description sounds somewhat hyperbolical, but indeed it is the only way in which I can describe this woman, whose every movement was full of sinuous grace and feline treachery. Cat, tigeress, pantheress as she was, her claws were now sheathed in her velvet paws, but the claws were there all the same, and would doubtless scratch at the least provocation.

Some people do not believe in transmigration, but I am a true disciple of Pythagoras in that bizarre doctrine, and I firmly believe that in a former existence the soul of Giulietta Morone had animated the body of some tawny tigeress who had stolen through the jungle beneath the burning skies of Hindostan, slaying and devouring her victims in conformity with the instincts of her savage nature. Now she was a woman—a fair, majestic woman—but the instinct of the beast was there, the desire for slaughter and the lust for blood. What made me indulge still more in this fancy was the colours of the dress she wore black and yellow—all twisted in and out with a curious resemblance to the sleek fur of the beast to which I had likened her. The soft glimmer of the pearl strings twined in her magnificent red hair seemed out of place as ornaments for this woman; but the rubies suited her nature well, the red, angry rubies that shot flashes of purple fire from her neck at every heave of her white bosom. Leaning back in her deep chair with a cruel smile on her full crimson lips, the glimmer of pearls, the fire-glint of the fierce-tinted gems, and the bizarre mixture of amber and black in her dress, she slowly waved her sandalwood fan to and fro, diffusing a strange, sleepy perfume through the room, and looking what I verily believed her to be, the type of incarnate evil in repose.

While I was thinking in this fanciful fashion, the Contessa was talking to her friends in a slow, rich voice, and Beltrami—well, Beltrami was watching me closely. Do you know that strange sensation of being watched? that uneasy consciousness that some unseen eye is observing the least movement? Yes, of course you do! Every one has felt it, in a more or less degree, according to their nervous susceptibility. At the present time, with all my senses on the alert for unexpected events, it was therefore little to be wondered at that I felt the magnetism of Beltrami's gaze, and, on looking up, saw his keen black eyes fixed upon me with an enigmatical expression. For the moment I was startled, but immediately that feeling passed away for I well knew the strange nature of the Marchese, which was a peculiar mixture of good and evil, of kindness and cruelty, of hate and love, which must have proceeded from some aberration of his subtle intellect.

Beltrami's face always put me in mind of that sinister countenance of Sigismondo Malatesta, which sneers so malevolently at the curious onlooker from the walls of the Duomo at Rimini. He had the same treacherous droop of the eyelids, the same thin nose with wide, sensitive nostrils, and the same malignant smile on his thin lips. Yet he was handsome enough, this young Italian; but his face, in spite of my friendship, repelled me—in a less degree, it is true, but still it repelled me in the like manner as did that of the Contessa Morone. So he was going to marry her. Well, they were certainly well-matched in every respect, and if the man had not the active wickedness of the woman, still the capability of evil was there, and would awaken to life when necessary to be exercised. Both Beltrami and his future wife were anachronisms in this nineteenth century, and should have lived, smiled, and died in the time of the Renaissance, when they would have been fitted companions of those Italian despots of whom Machiavelli gives the typical examples in his book "The Prince."

The Marchese saw my inquiring look, and with an enigmatic smile walked across to where I was standing in the warm, yellow light.

"Ebbene! Signor Hugo," he whispered, with a swift glance at the Contessa, "tell me what you think of my choice."

"It does you credit, Marchese. You will have a beautiful wife."

"And a loving one, I hope. Tell me, mon ami, do you not envy me?"

I hesitated a moment before replying, and then blurted out the truth,—

"Honestly speaking, Signor Luigi, I do not!"

"Dame! and why?"

"Well, I can hardly tell you my reasons, but I have them, nevertheless."

Beltrami looked hard at me with an inquisitive look in his dark eyes, and a satirical smile on his thin lips.

"You are not complimentary, my friend," he said, turning away with a supercilious laugh.

I laid my hand on his shoulder and explained,—

"Pardon me, Beltrami, you do not understand——"

"Eh! do not apologise! I understand better than you think."

He was evidently not at all offended, and I felt puzzled by his manner. It was true he had candidly acknowledged that he was making this marriage for money, but surely he must also love this woman, whose ripe beauty was so attractive to the passionate nature of the Italians. Yet, judging from his mode of speech, he evidently had some mistrust—a mistrust for which I could not account. He could know nothing of the affair at the Palazzo Morone, so there certainly could be no reason for suspicion on his part. She was a beautiful woman, a rich woman, an attractive woman, so with this trinity of perfections she decidedly merited a warmer love than Beltrami appeared inclined to give her. Could it be that her evil beauty repelled him, as it did me? No! that was impossible, seeing that, according to my idea, their natures were wonderfully alike. Altogether the whole demeanour of the Marchesa perplexed me by its strangeness, and I watched him narrowly as he approached the Contessa, to see if she perceived the lack of warmth on the part of her lover.

To my surprise, as he bent over her chair to speak, she shrank away with a gesture of disdain, and the rubies shot forth a red flame, as if to warn the lover that there was danger in pressing upon this woman his unwelcome attentions. Unwelcome, I am sure they were, for as he adjusted her cloak and aided her to rise, in order to return to the box, I saw that she accepted all his politeness with forced civility and cold smiles. So then she did not love him—he had almost openly acknowledged to me that he did not love her, and yet these two people, who had no feeling of love in their hearts, were about to marry. It was most extraordinary, and I marvelled greatly at the juxtaposition of these two human beings, who evidently hated one another heartily.

At this moment the Contessa spoke of the man she had murdered, and I was horrified in the cold, callous tones in which she veiled her iniquity.

"Do you know, gentlemen, if anything has been heard of this lost tenor?"

Beltrami shot a keen glance at her, then a second at me, and I felt more bewildered than ever by this strange action.

A Creature of the Night

"Nothing has been heard of him, Contessa," he said quickly, before the others could speak; "he has vanished altogether, but no doubt he will appear again."

"Ah, you think so?" observed the Contessa, with a cruel smile.

"I am sure of it!"

She winced, and looked at him in a startled manner, upon which, impelled by some mysterious impulse, I know not what, I joined in the conversation,—

"On the contrary, madame, I do not think Signor Pallanza will ever be seen again."

All present turned round in surprise, and the Contessa darted a look at me which seemed to pierce my soul. Only Beltrami was unmoved, and he, with a smile on his face, laid his hand upon my shoulder.

"Eh, Signor Hugo, and why do you think so?"

"A mere fancy, Marchese, nothing more."

"Ma foi! and a fancy that may turn out true!"

I was annoyed at having yielded to the impulse and spoken out, as, unless I told all about my adventure, I could not substantiate my statement, and I was certainly not going to reveal anything I knew, particularly in the presence of the woman so deeply implicated in the affair. Beltrami's mocking manner irritated me fearfully, the more so as it was so very unaccountable, and I was about to make some sharp reply, when the opening chorus of the last act sounded, and all the gentlemen, after making their adieux to the Contessa, left the room.

The Marchese offered his arm to Madame Morone, but she dismissed him with a haughty gesture.

"One moment, Marchese—I wish to speak with this Signor for a few minutes."

Beltrami darted one of his enigmatic looks at us both, and with a low bow to conceal the smile on his lips, left the room. As soon as he had disappeared, Madame Morone turned round on me with a quick gesture of surprise.

"Signor Hugo, why did you say the tenor Pallanza would never be seen again?"

"I have no reason, Signora," I replied, being determined to baffle her curiosity; "I merely spoke on the impulse of the moment."

"Do you know Signor Pallanza?"

"No, madame, I have not the pleasure of his acquaintance."

"Ah!"

She heaved a sigh of relief, and looked at me long and earnestly, as if to see whether I was speaking the truth. Apparently she was satisfied with her scrutiny, for she laughed softly, and placed her hand within my arm.

"Confess now, Signor Hugo, you think me most mysterious, but I will tell you why I speak thus. I heard Pallanza at Rome, when he sang at the Apollo, and I hoped to see him again here, therefore I am annoyed at his disappearance and anxious for him to be found. A selfish wish, Signor Hugo, for it is only my desire to hear him sing again. Ecco!"

"I do not think your wish at all selfish, madame, for I hear he is a charming singer."

"Oh, yes! the New Mario they call him in Milan. Will you not hear the rest of the opera in my box?"

"If you will excuse me, madame, I will say no, as I have an engagement."

This was a lie, but I was so fearful of betraying myself to this terrible woman, who had evidently a half-suspicion that I knew something of Pallanza, that I was anxious to get away as soon as possible. She, saying good-night, in a cold, polite manner, re-entered the box, and I was moving away when Beltrami suddenly appeared.

"Eh, Hugo, how cruel! the Contessa tells me you must go?"

"Yes. I will see you again, Marchese!"

"To-morrow then; if not, the next day. Here is my card, and I am always at home in the afternoon. Do not fail to come, mon ami—I wish to speak to you about—about——"

He paused, and I asked curiously,—

A Creature of the Night

"About what?"

"Eh, dame! I forget. I will tell you at our next meeting' A rivederci! Signor Hugo. Don't forget your old friend, or he will quarrel with you."

He nodded, smiled, and vanished, then I took my departure from the theatre, and wandered up and down the street in the moonlight. I felt that to sit out the ballet would be more than I could bear, as I was so excited over the meeting with the Contessa Morone, therefore I strolled up and down the street, smoking and thinking. As time passed on I grew calmer, and thought I would return to the Ezzelino, not to see the ballet, but to catch a glimpse of the Contessa once more.

As I reached the portico of the theatre she was just coming down the steps to her carriage, leaning on the arm of Beltrami, and I, hidden in the crowd, could see her looking hither and thither as if searching for some one. She could not see me, and in order to satisfy myself in every way as to her identity with the creature of the night I had seen leave the graveyard, with a sudden inspiration I hummed a few bars of the strange song I had heard in the fatal chamber.

Being close to me she could hear quite plainly, and gave a kind of gasping cry as she fell back into the arms of Beltrami, just as he was helping her into the carriage.

"What is the matter, cara?" he asked quickly.

She clutched his arm with so powerful a grasp that it made him wince, and I heard her mutter with white lips,—

"Pallanza! Pallanza!"

This was all I wanted to hear, and, fearful of discovery, I threaded my way quickly among the crowd, and hastened home to my hotel.

I had recognised Guiseppe, I had found the woman who had slain him, but I had yet to discover where she had hidden the body of her victim— and then!—well, my future movements would be guided by circumstances.

****

CHAPTER IX

FIORE DELLA CASA

I did not get much sleep that night after the excitements of the day, but towards the morning fell into an uneasy slumber, during which I had fragmentary dreams in which Pallanza, the Contessa, and the antique chamber were all mixed up together. One moment I was at the iron door of the tomb, and the guardian angel took the semblance of Signora Morone; the next I was kneeling beside the corpse of Pallanza, illuminated by the faint light of the candles; and I ever saw the pallid shade of Donna Renata pointing towards the watchful face of her husband, filled with ghastly meanings in the dim shadows. No wonder, after these terrific visions which blended the real and the ideal, I awoke in the grey morning light unrefreshed and haggard; so when the waiter brought me my roll and coffee I left them untouched, and, lying quietly in bed, wondered what step it was necessary to take next in solving this riddle.

Riddle do I say? No! it was a riddle no longer, save as to the visit of the Contessa to the vault of her family, for otherwise everything was clear enough. She had met Pallanza at Rome, and had fallen in love with his handsome face. The young man, flattered by the attentions of a great lady, had yielded readily enough to the charm of the situation, but, growing tired of the intrigue, had come to Verona, where Bianca awaited him, with the intention of breaking it off. With a woman of Giulietta Morone's fiery nature the sequel can easily be guessed—she had followed him hither, and having in some way forced him to come to the deserted palace, had there poisoned him out of revenge for his contemplated infidelity.

Of course, this was all theoretical, but from one thing and another I guessed that this could be the only feasible way of accounting for the whole affair. Two points, however, remained to be cleared up before the reading of the riddle could be successfully accomplished: the first being the reason of the burial-ground episode, the second the strange disappearance of the dead man's body.

In thinking over the legend related by Peppino, one thing struck me as peculiar—that Donna Renata had never been seen again after her husband entered the chamber, and I guessed from this that there was some secret oubliette or alcove in the room, with a concealed entrance in which Mastino Morone had entombed his guilty wife as a punishment for her crimes. Doubtless, from tradition or from old family papers, Madame Morone knew of this secret hiding-place, and having killed Pallanza, had put his body therein so as to destroy all evidences of her criminality. No one had seen Pallanza enter this deserted palace, so once his body was hidden in the secret alcove it would remain there for ever undiscovered, and no human being, save the Contessa herself, could ever tell what had become of him. She, for her own sake, would remain silent, and thus Guiseppe Pallanza's fate would remain a mystery for evermore.

Fortunately, however, God, who had thus permitted this evil woman to conceive and carry out her crime, had also permitted me to behold the murder, so that, secure as she no doubt felt of her safety, yet one word from me and the whole affair would be revealed. I never thought, however, of going to the Veronese police and telling them what I had seen, as in their suspicions of foreigners they would doubtless regard me as an accessory, and thus I would get myself into trouble, which I had no desire to do. I therefore determined to once more go to the fatal chamber and make a final effort to discover what had become of the body of the unfortunate Pallanza.

So far so good, but now the question arose, how much of this story was I to reveal to Bianca? I could not tell her the whole, for if the body of her lover were discovered, the poor child would suffer quite enough without the additional information of Guiseppe's infidelity; so, making a virtue of necessity, I determined upon telling her a pious lie. To do this it was necessary to leave out the Contessa Morone altogether, as the least mention of a woman's name would arose Bianca's suspicions, and for the Contessa I substituted a robber, who had decoyed Guiseppe to the deserted palace by means of a false letter, and there ended his life. Of course it was somewhat difficult to be consistent in the narrative; but I was so anxious to hide the cruel truth of Pallanza's worthlessness from Bianca that I went over the story I had invented, again and again, until I thought I had the whole pious fraud quite perfect.

Having thus arranged my plans, I arose, finished my roll and coffee, then, having dressed myself rapidly, set off at once for the Casa Angello, as it was nearly time for my lesson. All my bruises were now quite well, yet I felt very depressed and downcast, as the state of nervous excitement which I had been in for the last few days had told terribly on my system. However, having once put my hand to the plough I could not, with satisfaction to myself, turn back; and although I heartily dreaded the coming interview with Bianca, yet it was unavoidable, as the poor child was so anxious over her lost lover that it was necessary to tell my fictitious story without delay in order to set her mind at rest.

On my arrival at the Casa Angello I found no one there but Bianca, who was anxiously awaiting me. It appeared that the Maestro had taken it into his head that he would like a walk in the sunshine, and had gone out under the care of Petronella; but, as Bianca knew I was coming to take my usual lesson, and was anxious to hear if I had any news of her lover, she remained indoors to speak to me.

The "Fiorè della Casa," as old Petronella tenderly called her in the poetic language of the Italians, looked even paler than usual, and the dark shadows under her dark eyes made them appear wonderfully large and star-like. She had a bunch of delicate lilies-of-the-valley in the bosom of her white dress, and she looked as pale and blanched as the frail flowers themselves. Lying back on the green-covered sofa on which she was seated, she reminded me of a late snowflake resting on the emerald grass of early spring, which at any moment might vanish under the pale rays of the sun.

A Creature of the Night

We were talking together in the room in which I generally had my lessons, and my eyes wandered from one thing to another with vague hesitation as I looked everywhere but on the face of this delicate girl to whom I had to tell such a cruel story—for, soften it as I might, the story was cruel and could not fail to affect her terribly. Every object in the apartment photographed itself on my memory with terrible distinctness, and, even after the lapse of years, by simply closing my eyes I can recall the whole scene with the utmost truthfulness. The dull red of the terra-cotta floor, the heavy time-worn furniture, covered with faded green rep, the small ebony piano with its glistening white keys alternating with the black, the mirror-fronted press in which Petronella kept everything from food to clothes, the many photographs of operatic celebrities, and the gaudily painted picture of St. Paul, the Maestro's patron saint, encircled by a faded wreath of withered laurel-leaves and dead flowers, flung to some favourite pupil in her hour of triumph. Even the view from the window I can recall, with the slender campanile tower, from whence every quarter rang the brazen bells, and then the faltering voice of Bianca, "Fiorè della Casa," stealing like a melancholy wind through the silence of the room.

"Signor!" she said, twisting her thin white hands nervously together, "you have something to tell me of Guiseppe. I can see it in your face—is it good or evil?"

"What does my face tell you, Signorina?"

"Evil, evil! your eyes are sad, your mouth does not smile! Oh, tell me quickly what you know! Is he found? is he ill? is he—dead?"

She brought out the last word in a shrill scream, with dilated eyes that almost terrified me by the fear expressed in them, and, dreading the effect of a sudden shock on this fragile child, I hastily replied in the negative.

"No, Signorina, no! Do not look so fearful, I pray you. He is not dead. Child, I am sure he is not dead!"

"Then you have not found him yet?"

"No; I have not found him, but I think I know where he is to be found."

"What do you mean, Signor Hugo, tell me all—tell me all. See, I am strong, I can bear it—I wish to know everything."

"Signorina, the note which Guiseppe Pallanza received at the Ezzelino was not from a friend but from an enemy."

"An enemy!"

"Yes! from one who wished him ill. Thinking it was from his dying friend, he obeyed the letter and was lured to the deserted Palazzo Morone."

"I do not know that palazzo, Signor. I am a stranger in Verona."

"I know where it is, Signorina, for on that night I was wandering about near it, when I saw Pallanza go into it alone. Knowing the evil reputation of the place, I followed him, although he was a stranger to me. He went to a room in the palace where his enemy met him, and—and——"

"Yes! yes, Signor—for the love of the Saints, go on."

"I can tell you no more, Signorina, except that I do not believe Guiseppe left that room again. I believe he is there still, perhaps held captive by the robber who lured him thither in the hope of obtaining a ransom."

Bianca looked at me searchingly. She was a simple little thing as a rule, but this ridiculous story I had manufactured of brigands in the heart of Verona was too much even for her confiding nature, and she made a gesture of disbelief.

"It is not true! it is not true!" she cried vehemently. "Why do you deceive me, Signor?"

"I am not deceiving you."

"An enemy! a false letter! a deserted palace! held captive! Oh, I cannot believe it. If it is true, why did you not rescue him?"

"Because some one I do not know seized me from behind as I watched, and, rendering me insensible with chloroform, bore me away from the palace. I had great difficulty in finding it again, I assure you."

"Signor, your story is that of a dream. I cannot believe you."

"It is true, nevertheless."

Bianca said nothing, but tapped her little foot on the ground with a thoughtful frown on her small face. I was glad that my task was over, for absurd as was the story I had told her, it was more merciful than the truth. Now that I had to some extent quieted her fears by telling her that Guiseppe was alive—a thing, alas! that I could not be certain of myself—I hoped to get away at once to the Palazzo Morone and make one last effort to find his body. If I failed there would be nothing left for me to do but to inform the police, and in the interests of Bianca I was unwilling to do this until I had exhausted every means of solving the mystery myself.

Suddenly Bianca's face cleared, and she looked at me with steady determination.

"Signor, you know this palazzo?"

"Yes, Signorina."

"And this room where you think Guiseppe is held captive?"

"I do, Signorina."

"Then take me to it at once."

She started to her feet with a deep flush on her face, and threw out her hands towards me with an appealing gesture. As for me, I sat still, transfixed with astonishment at the spirit displayed by this gentle girl, who was thus willing to dare the dangers, of the unknown in order to save her lover.

"Take me to it at once!" she repeated quickly.

"Signorina, I—I cannot. You are mad to think of such a thing."

"Is your story true or false, Signor Hugo?"

"True! yes, it is true!"

"Then I will judge of its truth myself—with my own eyes. Wait, I will put on my hat, and you will take me to this palazzo at once."

"Signorina——"

"Not another word, I have made up my mind. You promised to be my friend, Signor Hugo. I hold you to that promise. Ecco!"

She was gone before I could utter further remonstrance, and during her absence I reflected rapidly. It was true that Guiseppe was dead, that I believed his body was concealed somewhere in that room, so perhaps after all it was best that Bianca should come, as her quick woman's wit might succeed where I had failed. She knew nothing about the implication of the Contessa Morone in the affair, the palazzo would be quite deserted during the daytime, so I would be able to take her there, let her examine the room, and if by chance the truth was revealed that Guiseppe was dead, it would be a more merciful way than by the lips of a stranger. Yes, I would take her there at once. If we failed in our mission she would be no wiser than before, but if we succeeded—ah! how I pitied the poor child if we succeeded in finding out the terrible secret of the Contessa. At this moment she returned trembling with ill-suppressed excitement.

"Well, Signor Hugo, are you ready—are you willing to help me?"

"With all my heart, Signorina."

"Ebbene! come, then."

She ran lightly out of the room, and I followed with a heavy heart, for I had a presentiment of evil. I feared that fatal chamber, which held so many impure memories—I feared the discovery of the dead—I feared for this child who went forward in ignorance to face such horrors.

***

CHAPTER X

A VOICE IN THE DARKNESS

On returning from my last visit to the palace I had carefully noted the way thereto, so I was able to escort Signorina Angello without calling in the services of Peppino. I was unwilling to drive there, as the presence of a fiacre even in that deserted piazza might be noticed, and I did not want any comment made by the scandal-loving Italian populace on our visit to this out-of-the-way locality. So in company with Bianca, who had put on a veil, and who said nothing to me from the time we left Casa Angello, being apparently occupied with her own reflections, I walked down the gloomy, narrow streets towards that terrible Palazzo Morone, the very idea of which inspired me with horror and dismay.

It was one of those burning days common to that time of the year in Italy, and much as I despised and cursed those drain-like alleys in wet weather, yet I now saw there was method in the madness of their style of building, for their cool shadow and humid atmosphere was wonderfully pleasant after the glare, the dust, and heat of the great piazza. We walked on the broad carriage-way, which was less painful to the feet than the cobble-stone paving between, and every now and then saw some typical picture of Italian life. A dark-faced woman with a red handkerchief twisted carelessly round her head, leaning from a high balcony, on the iron railings of which was displayed the family washing; a purple cloud of wisteria blooming in some pergola near the red roof-tops; sleek grey donkeys laden with panniers, stepping complacently along the narrow way; slender Italian men presiding over fruit-stalls, piled high with their picturesque contents; and over all, the vivacious clatter and din of voices, struck through at times with the sharp, metallic notes of the mandolin. It was very charming, and, I would have enjoyed it thoroughly, artistically speaking, had it not been for the local odours. Oh, the smells of those picturesque streets! they were too terrible for description; and how the Italians are not swept off the face of the earth by a plague of typhoid is more than I can understand. I smoked cigarettes most of the time, as a preventive against infection; but on beholding ideal paintings of Italian scenes, I always shudder at the memory of the malodorous reality, and on arriving in well-drained London again, my first prayer was one of thanks for having escaped from ill-smelling Italy.

My thoughts during this portentous walk were, I am afraid, rather frivolous; but so fearful had been the strain on my nerves for the past few days, that it was a great relief to think idly of anything and any one. Not so Bianca; even through her veil I could see the glisten of tears, and catch the sound of her quick indrawn breath as she strove to fight down the emotion that threatened to overwhelm her. I saw that the poor child was nearly hysterical with her efforts to control herself, and stopped short in dismay.

"Signorina, you are not well. Do not go to this palazzo."

"Yes, yes! I must, Signor Hugo. I cannot pass another night in this state of suspense. I must know all, and at once. Is the Palazzo Morone far off?"

"We are just at it, Signorina."

And so we were; for at that moment we entered the silent, grass-grown square, at the end of which stood the palazzo, looking gruesome even in the sunshine, with its broken windows, damp, disfigured walls, and general air of weird solitude. Some swallows were shooting through the still air and twittering round the rich sculptures of the façade, but their merry chirpings only added to the eerie feeling inspired by the great mansion—a feeling which I noticed thrilled Bianca with fear as she paused shuddering, under the grinning masks and unlovely faces peering downward from the arched entrance.

A Creature of the Night

"Oh, how could he come to this terrible place at night!" she cried, crossing herself, with a look of fear in her eyes. "Desolate as it is in the sun, what must it be when the moon shines! It is an abode of the dead—a tomb—a tomb! Dio! his tomb."

"Signorina, do not affright yourself thus! Things may not be so bad as you think."

"It is like the Inferno of Dante! and turns my blood cold with fear; but I will not go back! I must find Guiseppe, even if it cost me my life. Come, Signor, presto! there is no time to lose."

She crossed herself once more, then flitted through the opening in the iron gate like a noiseless-winged bird, upon which I hastily followed her, and we stood for a moment in the lonely courtyard, gazing at the great portals of the door leading to the hall, which stood half-open.

"Signorina, I will lead you to the room. You are not afraid? You do not tremble?"

"Ah! I am afraid, and I do tremble, Signor, for I am only a girl; but lead on, love will make me strong, and you will protect me. Give me your hand, Signor; I am not afraid when I hold your hand."

With a fleeting smile on her pale lips, she placed her hand in mine, and as I grasped its cold whiteness, I guessed how terrified this delicate, superstitious girl was of this unholy place. But for the resolute look on her pallid face, I would have insisted upon her turning back; but it was useless to urge retreat now, so with the name "Guiseppe! Guiseppe!" on her lips, as if to inspire her with courage, she almost dragged me through the half-closed door into the hall of shadows.

"Ah! Mother Mary, it is like a church!"

It was like a church—like some old deserted church, filled with the chill atmosphere of the grave; and the slow movement of the wind-shaken tapestries, the glimmer of the ghostly white stairs in the dim distance, and the solemnity of the huge pillars of black marble, made me think of those God-cursed cities of the "Thousand and One Nights," whose silence is only broken by the voice of the one survivor chanting the melancholy verses of the Koran. Bianca, overpowered by this mute spectacle of a dead past, clung convulsively to my arm with faltering prayers on her lips, and I became afraid lest, by a feeling of sympathy, her terror should unnerve me also, so with a cheerful laugh, which echoed dismally through the vast vestibule, I led her onward towards the grand staircase.

"Come, Signorina, do not be afraid. You are quite safe with me."

"Yes, yes! Guiseppe! Guiseppe!"

We slowly ascended the staircase, gained the corridor, and at length arrived at the second flight of shallow steps leading to the secret room. Here Bianca, seeing the darkness, nearly fainted with nervous fear, for, deeply imbued with grim Italian superstitions, she beheld unseen terrors in every shadowy corner. I again wanted her to return, but with wilful obstinacy she refused, so, as I luckily had a pocket-flask of brandy with me, I made her take a little to revive her. The fiery spirit put new life into her sinking limbs, and, after lighting my candle as usual, I led her up the steps, through the short corridor, through the tapestried ante-chamber, until at last we stood in the fatal room.

"Here, Signor Hugo!"

"Yes!"

She flung back her veil with a feverish gesture, and peered into the darkness, which was hardly broken by the feeble light of the small candle I carried. Suddenly a thought struck me which I at once put into execution, and lighted all the tapers yet remaining in the candelabra on the table. To the darkness succeeded a blaze of mellow light, and Bianca, with a look of surprise on her face, gazed round the singular room with the white pillars, the ominous blood-red hangings, and the banquet of the dead set forth with such splendid display on the gilt table.

"What a strange room!" she said timidly. "Signor Hugo! what does it mean?"

"I have told you all I know, Signorina. Your lover was lured to this room. I saw him pass through that door, and then I was drugged as I have said."

                                    A Creature of the Night

"You did not then see who received him here?"

"No! I did not."

The first part of the lie was difficult to utter on account of a choking feeling in my throat, but the last sentence came out with tolerable grace.

"And you do not think Guiseppe left this room again?"

"I'm afraid not, Signorina!"

"Then, where can he be?" she asked with an anxious look around.

"I think he is concealed in some secret cell, the entrance to which is from this apartment."

"Oh, Signor Hugo, let us look for it at once."

"Certainly!"

"A meal on the table—all this gold and silver. It is a robbers' cave, Signor."

"Y—es—I suppose so!"

"Come, let us be quick then, or the robbers may arrive."

She looked nervously towards the door, but I, taking a candle off the table, reassured her with a gay laugh,—

"Do not be afraid, Signorina. No one comes here during the day."

"Hush! what is that?"

Infected by her terror my heart gave a jump, and I listened intently, but could hear no sound.

"It is nothing, Signorina. Your nerves are unstrung!"

"No! No! I can hear it. Some one is coming. Listen!"

In order to humour her fancy I remained silent with all my senses on the alert, and with a feeling of dread I heard the sound. The light fall of footsteps, the rustle of a silken dress—a dress!—the full horror of the situation rushed on me at once.

"It must be the Contessa Morone!"

In a moment I had blown out all the candles, and, dragging Bianca with me, retreated in the darkness to the far end of the room. The girl gave a little cry as the lights disappeared, but I pressed her hand significantly.

"Hush, Signorina. Not a word!"

At the time I heard the steps they were at the door of the ante-chamber, where the new-comer was evidently pausing a moment, and as the curtains of the inner room had been half drawn aside on our entrance, it was for this reason we had heard them so clearly. The steps recommenced. I heard their soft, light fall on the marble floor, the rustle of the silken gown, like the sound of dry leaves in an autumnal wind, and then I felt that this woman was standing in the arched doorway, looking straight at myself and the shrinking girl through the darkness.

"Why are you here, Signor Hugo, and who is that woman?"

It was the voice of the Contessa, and I gave a cry of horror as I suddenly remembered how ineffectual the darkness was to conceal us from the eyes of this nyctalopist. Bianca, however, knew nothing of this woman, or of her gift of seeing in the dark; so, overcome with fear at the demoniac power she believed the unknown possessed, she gave a shriek of terror and sank fainting at my feet.

"What does this mean?"

Again the voice of the Contessa sounded cruel and menacing in its tones; so feeling myself at a disadvantage in the dark, through not possessing the terrible attribute of this woman, I staggered forward and lighted the candles. At once out of the gloom sprang that evil face with a frown on the white brow, a deadly glitter in the cruel eyes, and an ominous tightening of the thin lips.

I don't think I can call myself a coward, but at that moment my blood ran cold at the horror of that Medusa-like countenance, and I stood before this phantom of Lucrezia Borgia as if turned into stone, unable to move or speak.

The Contessa moved forward to the table and looked at me steadily, with a wicked smile frozen on her red lips.

"You do not reply, Signor Hugo; but I begin to understand. You have been here before?"

"Yes!"

I hardly recognised my own voice, so hoarse and broken did it sound, stealing in a whisper from between my dry lips. She still looked at me steadily, and I felt fascinated with dread by the snake-like glare of those cruel eyes.

"When were you here, Signor?"

"On Monday night!"

"And you saw—nothing," she said in a meaning tone.

"Yes!" I replied, lifting my head boldly, "I saw you receive Guiseppe Pallanza, and I saw you give him the poisoned cup!"

She gave a cry of rage like a trapped animal, and made a step forward, but restraining herself with a powerful effort, sank into a chair and leaned her elbow on the table. Dressed in heavy black garments of velvet and silk, she looked more like the Borgia than ever, and the ruby necklace she constantly wore flashed forth rays of red fire in the glimmer of the tremulous light.

"I understand now why you said Guiseppe Pallanza would not come back," she said with a scornful smile. "I thought last night you knew more than you told. Eh! Signor, and it was you who sang at the door of the Ezzelino."

"Yes, it was I."

"Meddlesome Englishman that you are, do you not fear that I will treat you as I treated that false one?"

"No! I mistrust your wine!"

"True, Signor Machiavella! forewarned is forearmed. So you came here to look for Pallanza?"

"I came to look for his body, Madame Morone, but I do not know where it is."

"No; nor will you find it. And who is this woman?"

"Guiseppe's betrothed."

The Contessa gave a cry of rage, and, rising from her seat, rushed towards the unconscious girl where she lay in the darkness. Owing to her singular gift she needed no light to see by, but examined the face of her rival minutely in the gloom. I had stepped forward, fearing lest, carried away by jealous anger, she should do the poor child an injury; but such was not her intention, for after a minute's examination, she arose from her stooping position with a burst of wicked laughter.

"So it was for this white-faced thing that he was going to leave me—me, Giulietta Morone! Eh, I feel much flattered at having such a rival. Why is she here, Signor Hugo?"

"To find Pallanza," I replied shortly.

"She will never find him; he is lost to her for ever. But," she added, with a wicked smile, "I am not afraid of your betraying me, Signor Hugo. I am not afraid of this poor fool, who thought to take Guiseppe from me, so I will revenge myself."

"Revenge yourself?"

"Yes; I have said it. You came here like a thief in the night, and saw what you were not meant to see. She comes in the daylight to seek her lover. Well, she shall see him. Wait till she revives, and I will blast her eyes with the sight of what he is now."

"You are a demon!"

"I am a wronged woman, whom a man sought to deceive. Ecco! Behold, then, Englishman that you are, how we Italian women revenge ourselves!"

She stepped past the unconscious body Of the girl, and, going to one of the pillars on the right side of the room, apparently touched a spring, for the whole pillar—which, as I have described before, was half built into the wall—revolved slowly with a grating sound and displayed a cavity. I bent forward with a shudder of horror, and saw—nothing!

The cavity was empty!

Signora Morone gazed at it with a look of horror on the wild beauty of her face; then, with a cry of rage, of fear, and of dread, rushed out of the room.

I heard her shriek, "Lost! lost! lost!" three times, then the sound of her retreating footsteps died away in the distance, and I was left alone in the ghastly gloom with the unconscious girl at my feet, and an agony in my heart such as I never hope to feel again in this life.

How I got out of that accursed room I hardly know; but I faintly remember lifting Bianca in my arms, and, guided by instinct, stagger through the dark corridors, down the silent stairs, and out into the courtyard. The fresh air seemed to revive me, and, collecting my scattered senses together with a gigantic effort, I looked round for some means by which to bring Bianca out of her faint, the length of which alarmed me terribly.

In the corner of the courtyard there was a sculptured trough, which the late rains had brimmed over, so, hastening towards this, I filled my cap with water, and, returning to Bianca, threw it in her face.

She revived slowly with a shuddering sigh, and looked round vacantly; then, with a sudden recollection of what she had come through, she flung herself into my arms with an imploring cry,—

"Oh, that voice! that voice! Take me away from that cruel voice!"

***

CHAPTER XI

THE MARCHESE BELTRAMI

I managed to take Bianca home without much difficulty, for it was my good fortune to meet a disengaged fiacre in one of the narrow streets leading to the piazza Vittorio Emanuele, and placing the poor girl therein, we drove straight to the Casa Angello. The Signorina was in a very excited state, as that menacing voice, issuing out of the darkness, had quite unnerved her; so, placing her in charge of Petronella, who made her lie down, I went for a doctor. Being a stranger in Verona it was difficult to find one, but at last I did so, and took him at once to see Bianca, for whom he prescribed a soothing draught, and assured me that she would be all right after a few hours' sleep. This trouble therefore being off my mind, I went back to my hotel, in order to consider what was best to be done in the present emergency.

I now saw that my surmise was right, and that the Contessa had hidden the body of the unfortunate Pallanza in the concealed tomb contrived by Count Mastino Morone for his guilty wife. It was a horribly ingenious idea that revolving pillar, and no one would have guessed its ghastly secret without being shown. Doubtless the wicked Donna Renata, shut up in this circular prison, had there starved slowly to death in an upright position, for, of course, the cavity was too narrow and too shallow to admit of any human being lying down. The skilful devilry of the device made me feel quite ill, especially when I thought how the worthy descendant of Borgia's accursed daughter had utilised this secret cell for her own infamous purpose. In this frightful oubliette the body of Guiseppe Pallanza would have remained for ever concealed; but then, according to the evidence of my own eyes, the body was not there.

That the Contessa had placed the corpse in the pillar I had not the slightest doubt, as in showing the hiding-place she evidently expected to overwhelm me by the hideous evidence of her barbarous criminality. That the cavity was empty was as much a surprise to her as to me, and the shriek of terror she had given when flying from the chamber showed me that she was overpowered with fear at the thought that her gruesome secret was shared by another person, for, putting me out of the question altogether, there appeared to be a third party implicated in this singular affair.

For my own part I believed it to be the man who had watched with me at the curtained archway, and who, after drugging me, bore me insensible from that terrible place. After doing so, and thus, according to his idea, putting it out of my power to re-discover the palace, he had returned to his post and seen the Contessa conceal the body of her victim in the cavity of the pillar. On her departure, for some reason best known to himself, he had removed the corpse, and hidden it somewhere else. This was, no doubt, the true story of the affair, but who was the man who had watched at the door, and who had taken away the body of Pallanza? It was impossible to guess the reasons for his behaving in this mysterious way, and the Contessa was evidently as ignorant as myself of his actions, judging from her terrified flight on discovering the truth. Whomsoever this unknown person was, he, to all appearances, held the key to the whole riddle, and, could I find him, I would doubtless learn the reason of Madame Morone's visit to the burial-ground, and the final fate of the unhappy tenor whom she had lured to his destruction.

But how to find him! that was the question, and one to which I could find no satisfactory answer; so in the dilemma in which I thus found myself involved, I decided to tell Luigi Beltrami, as the only friend I had in Verona, the whole devilish story. In addition to the desire I felt of asking his advice and opinion, I thought it but right that he should know the real character of the woman he was about to marry, and not discover too late that he was tied for life to a ghoul, a vampire, a murderess.

With this determination I looked for the card the Marchese had given me, and finding it in one of my pockets, discovered that my Italian friend lived in the Via Cartoni. As he had mentioned that he was always at home in the afternoon, doubtless to take a siesta during the heat of the day, on finishing my midday meal I went out to pay him a visit.

In spite of his assertion that he was poor, Beltrami had a sufficient income to warrant him living in a moderately expensive manner, and on my arrival at his rooms in the Via Cartoni, I was shown into a very well-furnished apartment. As the Marchese was stationed with his regiment at Verona for some considerable time, he had evidently brought a portion of his furniture from his Florentine palazzo, for the room was too handsome to be that of the ordinary class of furnished apartments. As usual, the ceiling was charmingly painted; the floor was of marble, covered here and therewith square Turkish carpets; and in addition to a piano there were plenty of pictures and photographs, showing the artistic taste of the owner of the place.

Beltrami himself, dressed as usual in his uniform, was seated at a desk placed in the window, writing letters, but he desisted when I was announced, and arose to greet me with marked cordiality.

"Ma foi, Hugo, this is kind of you to call so soon," he said when I was comfortably established in a chair. "I was just writing you a letter asking you to dine with me and go to the Ezzelino to-night, but as you are here the note is useless."

"The fact is, my dear Marchese, I have called on a selfish errand."

"Indeed!"

"Yes; still it is one that concerns yourself also."

"How so, mon ami? Come, tell me this mystery about which I know nothing and you know everything; but first here are some excellent cigarettes—Russian, my friend, not Italian. Dame! the tobacco of this country, it is horrible. Will you have some wine?"

"No, thank you, Beltrami, but I will be glad to smoke."

"Bene! help yourself."

                                                  A Creature of the Night

He pushed the box towards me, and, after I had taken a cigarette, followed my example, then, throwing himself into a chair near me, he nodded his head to show that he was ready to hear what I had to say.

"Marchese!" I said, after some slight hesitation, "I think we are old enough friends to admit of my speaking to you freely."

"Eh! certainly!"

"I trust you will not be offended."

Beltrami blew a wreath of smoke, and laying back his handsome head on the cushions of the chair, laughed heartily.

"No, my doubting Englishman, I promise you I will not be offended at anything you say."

"But, Luigi, it is about the Contessa Morone!"

"Eh! about the Contessa?—I thought as much!"

"How so?" I asked in some surprise.

The face of the Marchese assumed that cruel, cunning look I so much disliked to see, and he eyed me in a nonchalant manner.

"Dame! Signor Hugo, I will tell you when I hear your story of the Contessa."

Thus committed to narrative, I told Beltrami the whole story of my adventure from the time I had seen the Contessa at the graveyard to the hour when she had fled in dismay from the Palazzo Morone. He listened attentively, and when I had finished remained silent for a few minutes with a thoughtful look on his dark face.

"Why do you tell me all this, mon ami?" he asked, at length, twisting his moustache in a reflective manner.

"For two reasons. First, you may be able to aid me in my search for Pallanza; and second, you must have been ignorant of the character of the woman you are going to marry."

"As to the first reason, Hugo, you are right. As to the second, you are wrong."

"What, you know——"

"I know most of the story you have told me, and as to the Signora Morone, mon Dieu! I know her better than she does herself."

"Then why marry her?"

Beltrami shrugged his shoulders and selected another cigarette.

"Eh! she is rich and I am poor. It is time I ranged myself, as the French say, and I cannot afford to marry a poor wife; besides——"

"Besides what?"

"I rather like the task of taming this demon of a woman. Madame Morone is Satan's mistress in the matter of temper, I know, but I come of a race who either broke the will of their wives or——"

"Or?" I asked interrogatively.

"Or killed them!"

"That's rather risky nowadays, Marchese. We do not live in the time of the Renaissance remember. But let us leave off this discussion of Madame Morone. I have told you my story, and you say you knew most of it before!"

"And I say truly. Now listen, you cold-blooded islander, and see if I cannot disturb your phlegmatic disposition."

He paused a moment to give greater weight to his remarks, the conclusion of which I impatiently awaited.

"I was the man who drugged you and had you carried to the Piazza Vittorio."

"You!"

"I was the man who carried away the body of Guiseppe Pallanza."

"You!"

"I am the man who, knowing what I do, calmly and with open eyes, have made up my mind to marry Madame Morone."

"You!"

A Creature of the Night

I was so overwhelmed with the disclosures made by Beltrami that I could only sit thunderstruck in my chair, looking like an idiot and repeating "You! you! you!" parrot-fashion. Beltrami enjoyed my confusion for some time, and then went on speaking with a mocking smile:—

"Eh! I astonish you, Hugo. Well, I admit I treated you rather badly, my friend; but then at the time I did not know whom you were. Dame! I cannot see in the dark like Madame Gatta."

The Marchese then was the man who held the key to this enigma, and, far from being offended at his rough treatment of me on that fatal night, I was only too delighted at discovering the unknown person who, in this strange repetition of the old legend, had played the part of Count Mastino Morone.

"I have rather startled you, I fancy, Hugo?" said Beltrami with an ironical laugh.

"I would be a fool to deny it; but now that your dramatic surprise has come off so excellently, perhaps you will tell me what it all means."

"Without doubt; confidence for confidence! Besides, I want your help to carry this comedy to its legitimate conclusion."

"Comedy, you call it? To my mind it is more like a tragedy."

"There you are wrong, mon ami. In a tragedy there must be a death."

"Well! You forget Pallanza?"

"Not at all, Hugo; that is the whole point. Pallanza is not dead."

I stared at the Marchese in astonishment.

"Pallanza not dead! Impossible! I saw him die on that night."

"Dame! You saw him fall insensible at the feet of the Contessa Morone, but insensibility is not death."

"Then he is alive?"

"Naturally! One must either be alive or dead. And as this devil of a tenor is not the latter, he must therefore be the former."

"Then where is he?"

"Eh! that is part of the story."

This epigrammatic fencing on the part of Beltrami annoyed me greatly, as it piqued my curiosity without satisfying it, and I threw my half-smoked cigarette away with an outburst of bad temper.

"My dear Luigi, you have promised to tell me the story of this mystery, and instead of doing so you fire off epigrammatic squibs like Pasquin during the Carnival. The story, the story! I beg of you."

"Eh! certainly! Then take another cigarette, and I will tell you this 'Thousand and Second Night' romance."

***

A Creature of the Night

CHAPTER XII

DEATH IN LIFE

"It is such a long story, Hugo," said Beltrami, a trifle maliciously, "that we must really have some wine."

"I do not want wine; I want 'The Thousand and Second Night.'"

"Bene! you shall have both."

The Marchese arose and summoned his servant, who brought up a bottle of Barbera, that rough-tasting wine which is so pleasant and cool in hot weather. For the sake of companionship I took some with Beltrami, and having thus attended to the duties of hospitality, he signed to his servant to withdraw, and without further preamble began his tale.

"Eh, Hugo, mon ami," he said, settling himself comfortably in his chair, "this would be a charming story for M. Bourget, that modern Balzac, who analyses the hearts of the ladies of this generation in so masterly a fashion. Dame! I would like to give him Madame Morone's to dissect—he'd find some strange things there. Yet—would you believe it?—this woman, worthy to be a sister of Lucrezia Borgia, came out of a convent to marry my poor friend Morone."

"You knew him then?"

"Ma foi! I should think so, for many years. People said he was mad, but the only mad action he committed, to my mind, was in marrying Giulietta Rossana."

"Yet you propose to do the same thing?"

"True, but I possess a means of taming this tigress of which the unfortunate Giorgio Morone knew nothing. He was a great chemist, this poor Count, and particularly fond of toxicology, a dangerous science with such a wife, as he found out to his cost. Cospetto! I would not care myself about forging weapons for another to use against me, but that is exactly what Morone did."

"She poisoned him?"

"Eh! nobody says so, yet everybody thinks so. For my part, I believe the Contessa capable of anything. At all events, Morone died very suddenly, and was duly buried in that old ancestral vault to which his devoted wife, a year after his death, paid a visit. Well, before he died, Morone grew suspicious of the Contessa, and as he had just invented or rediscovered a poison which left no trace of having been used, and also an antidote to the same, he determined not to give the Signora an opportunity of exercising it on him, so this toxicological secret was buried with him."

"Ah! I see now why she went to the graveyard. It was to get this poison."

"Exactly! Whether it was put in the coffin of the dead man, or merely hidden in the vault, I don't know, but we will go and see."

"To what end? She has the poison!"

"Certainly! I believe that, after seeing it exercised upon Pallanza; but she has not got the antidote."

"How do you know that, Beltrami."

"Because the Contessa knows nothing of the existence of the antidote. Morone talked enough about the poison itself, but he only mentioned the antidote to one man, and that was myself. You see, Hugo, he thought madame might try a little of his own poison on himself, in which case I would be able to give him the antidote."

"Couldn't he have taken it himself?"

"No! this poison does not kill unless given in a large quantity; five drops make you feel chill and listless; ten drops take away your senses and converts you into what I may paradoxically call a breathing corpse; but fifteen drops kill. So, if madame had given her husband fifteen drops he would have lapsed into a stupor and died, unless the antidote was given, so that is why he bestowed it on me."

"Well, but she killed him after all?"

"Yes, but with another poison not of home manufacture. Eh! what would you, Hugo, the Contessa was not going to be thwarted by a husband who kept his laboratory locked. However, he tricked her over this particular poison, for he either gave instructions that it was to be put into his coffin without the knowledge of his dear wife, or he hid it himself in the vault, as he hinted to me one day he intended to do."

"There's no doubt then that the Contessa went to the vault for the poison; but what about the antidote? Is it in your possession?"

"Unfortunately, no, mon ami. I was ordered away from Verona, and gave back the antidote to the Count; but on my return here, I heard casually that he had left a letter for me, to be delivered after his death. I went to Rome, where the Contessa was one of the ornaments of the Court, and asked for the letter. Of course she denied ever having heard of it."

"And what do you think was in this letter?"

"Eh! ma foi, I believe it told me where the poison was hidden in the vault, and that our dear Contessa found the letter, went to the vault on the night you saw her and obtained the poison."

"Also the antidote?"

"Dame! I'm not so sure of that. I knew about the antidote so well that I don't think Morone would have mentioned it in the letter, in case it should meet the eye of his wife. No! No! mon ami! she has the poison, of course; but the antidote, I believe it is still in the vault, where we will look for it."

"For what reason?"

"Diamine! to revive this devil of a tenor who has had the misfortune to take ten drops of the Signora Morone's mixture."

"But where is Pallanza?"

"All in good time, Hugo, all in good time. I must tell you the rest of the story first."

"I am all impatience, Beltrami."

The Marchese, I saw, was enjoying this conversation, as the subject-matter was of an involved and difficult character which appealed to the subtleties of his Italian nature; and the chance of playing a part in this intrigue, worthy of the Court of Lorenzo di Medici, delighted him beyond measure. He was, as I have said before, an anachronism, and this everyday, commonplace life of the nineteenth century offered no field for the exercise of his cunning brain and delicate diplomacy, which revelled in those bizarre complications, full of sophistry and double meanings, which distinguished the intricate statecraft of the Italian republics.

"You wonder," continued the Marchese reflectively; "you wonder, no doubt, after hearing my opinions about the Contessa Morone, that I should care to marry her; but, as I told you before, there are reasons. I am poor, she is rich, and I marry her for her money. This is brutal is it not? but then you see I look at the matter from a Latin point of view, you from an English. As Euclid—whom, by the way, I always hated—says, 'Two parallel straight lines cannot meet,' it is no use our arguing over this point, as neither of us would convince the other. It is a question of race, Hugo, nothing more. Ebbene! my other reason is that I wish to tame this woman with the heart of a tigress. I am wearied of the dulness of this present life, and the task of fencing with Signora Morone will be a perpetual excitement, particularly as I know it will not be unattended with danger. This is also a question of race, and the theory of straight lines applies, so again we will not argue; but you can see one thing plainly, that I want to marry the Contessa?"

"Yes, I can see that, and I wonder at your daring."

"Straight lines, for the third time, Signor Hugo. Ebbene! Although I wanted to marry the Contessa, she hating and detesting me with her whole soul, as a friend of her late husband, would not listen to me at all, so as she would not go to the altar willingly, I determined to force her there. I made it my business to find out all about her life, and a devil of a life it is, I can tell you. Pallanza is not the first lover this daughter of Venus has smiled on."

"Oh!" I broke out in disgust, "how can you think of marrying this infamous woman—a murderess, a poisoner, a fiend in human form?"

"Dio! I have given you my reasons, and you, straitlaced Englishman that you are, cannot understand them. However, we will talk of this again; meantime to continue. The Contessa was so madly in love with Pallanza, who I grant you is a handsome fellow with a charming voice, that I foresaw when he attempted to leave her there would be trouble. I discovered that he was engaged to some Signorina of Milan, that she was at Verona, and that Pallanza was going to sing at Verona; so when he did arrive I was in nowise astonished at the appearance of Madame Morone at the Ezzelino. Things were coming to a climax, so I watched for the bursting of the storm. The rendezvous of these lovers would be, I knew, at the deserted Palazzo Morone. How did I know? Mon cher ami, you are simplicity itself. Have I not told you that I knew the Contessa when she lived at Verona with her husband, and—and—well it is not the first time she has used that palazzo and played at Boccaccian stories in that room. You know she fancies herself like Lucrezia Borgia, and tries to imitate those picturesque feasts to which Ferrara's Duchess was so addicted—yes, even to the use of poison. Dame! I thought I was at the opera when I saw that supper the other night."

"How did you get into the palazzo?"

"Ah, that is an adventure worthy of Gil Bias. I filed through a bar in the gate and wrenched it out."

"I thought so, for I entered the same way!"

"I guessed as much, my friend. Ebbene! I watched the palace from the time Madame Morone arrived in Verona, and my patience was rewarded on Monday night by seeing our picturesque tenor use his key and enter by the side door. I was not alone, for I greatly mistrusted Madame Morone should she discover me in that lonely palazzo; so, as

I had two men absolutely devoted to me, I took them with me."

"They were very brave to go near that ghastly palace, considering the reputation it has."

"Ma foi, they are Florentines, and know nothing about Verona. Their ancestors have been in the service of mine for many years, and in their eyes a Beltrami can do no wrong. Now is that not wonderful in this present age of ducats and steam-engines?"

"So wonderful, Marchese, that I can hardly believe it!"

"Cospetto! it is true I tell you. These men are absolutely devoted to me, and think me a much greater man than Umberto of Savoy. Ebbene! I posted my two men in a dark corner of the palazzo with instructions not to move until I told them; then I went after our tenor, and found him strumming on the mandolin while he awaited the arrival of the Contessa."

"Ah! she had gone to the burial-ground."

"Yes! I did not know that until you told me. However, I hid myself behind the tapestry in the outer room and waited. The Contessa arrived, and, to my surprise, you also appeared. I caught a glimpse of you at the door before that torch went out, but, of course, I did not recognise you, and was puzzled to account for your presence there. Luckily, I had a bottle of chloroform in my pocket, which I took with me to the palace in case of accidents——"

"But what good would chloroform do?"

"Dame! have you ever seen Madame Morone in a rage?"

"No!"

"Then it is not a pretty sight, I can tell you. That woman is a devil, and, for all I know, might have had some one in the palace to do her bidding. If I had been found there, and taken at a disadvantage, I might have occupied that delightful pillar and never been seen again. Ah! you smile, mon ami, but remember this is Italy, not England, and with a woman like the Contessa, who recalls the Borgia times so admirably, it is always well to be prepared If she had discovered me, my chloroform might have come in useful."

"It certainly did in my case!"

"Ma foi, I've told you before I did not know it was you. I only beheld a stranger, and thinking that the stranger might interfere with my plans, I stole across the ante-chamber, and when you fell back—well, I used my chloroform. Then I left you lying hidden behind the tapestry, and went on watching Madame Morone at her Borgian supper. She was dragging Pallanza's body to the pillar, and, having safely shut him up there, departed with a satisfied smile on her face; so I was left alone with two apparently dead men—Pallanza in the pillar, and you behind the tapestry."

"A sufficiently dramatic situation I think, Marchese."

"Eh! no doubt. There is more drama in life—-especially in Italian life—than people think, and there are even stranger events than this comedy of the Palazzo Morone take place in our midst."

"From what I have seen of your people, Luigi, I quite believe it. Well, about this dramatic situation—what did you do next?"

"Cospetto! I played my part on the stage with great judgment, I can tell you. When I was sure that Madame Morone had left the palazzo I re-lighted the candles, and went to see what appearance my man behind the tapestry presented. To my surprise I recognised Signor Hugo Cranston, and you may fancy I was considerably astonished, as I could not understand how you had become mixed up in this Boccaccian adventure. Friendship said, 'Revive him and apologize.' Caution remarked, 'Remove him from the palazzo, and let him think the events of the night a dream.'"

"Oh! and you adopted the advice of caution?"

"Diavolo! what else could I do? You might have interfered with my plans; and, besides, I always intended to give you an explanation when the Contessa became the Marchesa Beltrami. Circumstances, however, have brought about the explanation sooner than I intended."

"So I see," I replied drily. "However, you removed me from the palace."

"Yes! I called up my two men, and, telling them you were—well—overcome by Bacchus, ordered them to take you to the Piazza Vittorio

Emanuele and leave you there. Ecco!"

"Oh, Beltrami."

"Eh, you reproach me. Well, I no doubt deserve your reproaches, but it was the best excuse I could think of, as it doesn't do to trust servants too much. Ebbene! they took you away and left you in the Piazza, where you awoke in the morning?"

"I did, with a confounded headache."

"Ma foi! that was the chloroform, no doubt. Having thus arranged your little matter I went to the pillar and released Guiseppe Pallanza."

"He was not dead, then?"

"No! She gave him ten drops, I tell you. So that, although he was not actually dead, he had all the appearance of a corpse. I could not revive him as I had not the antidote; so, when my two men returned, I had him brought here."

"Here! In this house?"

"Precisely! he is in the next room. We will go and look at him presently. But to continue: the next day I called upon the Contessa, and told her I had seen all, suppressing, however, the fact that I had carried off this unfortunate lover."

"Which accounted for her surprise to-day on seeing the pillar empty?"

"Of course; she never dreamed that I would meddle with her work. Well, I gave her a choice of either explaining her little adventure to the authorities, and thus run a chance of being imprisoned for life, or of becoming my wife. Of these two evils she chose the least; so now I am engaged to marry her, and she will become the Marchesa Beltrami next month. Interesting, is it not, Hugo?"

It was no use arguing with this man, who, as he said himself, looked at the affair in a totally different light from what I did, and I did not know whether to loathe his brutal candour, to despise his mercenary designs, or to admire his undoubted courage in marrying this woman. However, I reflected that his subtle intriguing would undoubtedly be

A Creature of the Night

sufficiently punished by his marriage with this tigress of a Contessa, and as my only desire was to restore Pallanza to the arms of Bianca, I neither condemned nor praised Beltrami's singular conduct, which seemed admirable in his own eyes, but simply complimented him on his adroitness in following the precepts of Niccolo Machiavelli. He listened to my cold remarks with a disbelieving smile on his face, and laughed mockingly when I ceased speaking.

"Eh! Hugo, you do not approve of my ideas? Well, I do not wonder at that Fire and water are not more different than an Italian and an Englishman. Your cool blood comes from generations of church-going, straight-laced ancestors, whose beliefs ruled their lives in a simple manner; but my fiery blood burned in the veins of those condottieri of the Renaissance who were at war with King and Pope and Republic, who constantly stood on the verge of unseen precipices, and who needed all their craft, their courage, and their iron nerve to preserve their lives and fortunes. Dame! let us talk no more of such contrasts, but come with me, and I will show you this missing lover of Madame Morone."

I acquiesced eagerly in this proposal, and followed Beltrami, who led me into his bedroom, and, having unlocked a door in the opposite wall, ushered me into a small, bare apartment, containing a bed on which lay the still form of Guiseppe Pallanza. There he was dressed the same as on that fatal night, with his eyes closed, a frozen look on his white face, and his hands crossed on his breast. Lying thus in his antique garb he put me in mind of one of those coloured statues which adorn the tombs of great men; where the face, the hair, and the vestments are all tinted so as to produce the semblance of life. But was life here, in the body of this young man, who lay so passively before me with closed eyes as though he were indeed buried in some sepulchre of the dead?

"Oh! he is alive," said Beltrami, guessing my thought as I shrank back from the bed; "it is a case of suspended animation."

"But lasting three——four days?"

"Dame, yes! It would last much longer, I have no doubt. Ten drops produce this life-in-death state which you see, fifteen drops the same thing; but the one ends in death after a certain time, the other does not."

"But why did you not go to the vault and find this antidote at once?"

"Well, to tell you the truth, Hugo, I thought it would be a useless errand, as I do not know where to look for it. I fancied that Madame Morone might have found another bottle of this damnable poison, but it never struck me until I heard your story that she had read the letter addressed by Morone to me, and gone to the vault for the poison."

"And what are we to do now?"

"Go to the vault, to be sure, and look for this antidote."

"But, the vault is locked!"

"True, I forgot that," said Beltrami, with a thoughtful frown, "however, I think I can procure the key."

"From Madame Morone?"

"Dame! No! that would put her on her guard at once. I want her to think Pallanza is still in this cataleptic state, otherwise she won't marry me, as my power over her will be gone. I'll get the key somehow; if not, one of my men knows something about picking locks, so we will take him with us."

"A reputable servant, truly!"

"Eh! What would you!" said Beltrami carelessly, as he led the way out of the room and locked the door. "Even lock-picking is useful on occasions—witness the present one. Well, are you ready to go to the vault with me to-night?"

"At night, Beltrami?"

"Most certainly. If we went in the daytime all Verona would be in commotion. No! we must go at midnight when no one is about. Have you the courage?"

"I think so! but I hope Madame Morone will not be there!"

"There's no fear of that, as she has no reason to pay a second visit to the remains of her husband. She has got the poison, and knows nothing about the antidote, so make yourself easy on that score. Ecco!"

"What are you going to do now, Marchesa!"

"See if I can obtain that key. If I fail to obtain it, I will bring Matteo with me. As for you, my friend, go and take something to eat, and meet me on the Ponte Aleardi at midnight."

"I will be there, Beltrami. Good-bye for the present."

"À revederci, Hugo; I am obliged for your confidence, as it has solved the difficulty of knowing what to do with Signor Cupid."

We both went different ways; Beltrami to search for his key, and myself to hasten home to my hotel, and prepare myself for the fatigues of this midnight excursion, which, however much it appealed to the Marchese's sense of the romantic, was certainly not relished by me.

***

CHAPTER XIII

"DOWN AMONG THE DEAD MEN."

Do you know that gruesome old ballad, with its sombre refrain of "Down! Down! Down among the dead men?" A friend of mine with a deep bass voice, used to sing it in order to display his lower notes, upon which—and not without reason—he flattered himself greatly; but in after years, I never heard it sung without a shudder, so vividly did it recall to my mind the grotesque horror of that midnight visit to the Tomb of the Morone, in that old burial-ground of Verona. Of late I had been so much mixed up with ghosts, vaults, ghouls and crimes, that I was by no means anxious to continue the category, and would have infinitely preferred to have let Beltrami, who liked such uncomfortable things, go alone; but being an Englishman, I had to uphold the honour of my country, so never thought for a moment of showing the white feather. Besides, the only chance of saving Pallanza was by obtaining possession of the antidote, and in spite of my repugnance to the errand, I fully made up my mind to be on the Ponte Aleardi at the appointed time.

Meanwhile I fortified myself against possible horrors by having an excellent dinner, supplemented by a small bottle of champagne. I could not afford that luxurious wine, and it was sinfully extravagant of me to waste my small stock of money upon such a thing, but in the face of this midnight adventure I really felt that a little stimulant would comfort me under the circumstances. The result was admirable, for all my nervous apprehensions disappeared, and I sat in the smoking-room puffing at my after-dinner pipe in a very contented frame of mind, considering what awaited me at twelve o'clock p.m. Was I a coward? I don't think so. Many men who have no physical fear, and would ride gaily enough into battle, shrink with superstitious awe from the eerie neighbourhood of the dead, and I, owing to the causes I have stated before, am of this class. Come, then, ye dauntless scoffers, who would dare anything—in the broad daylight, and let me see if you would contemplate a midnight visit to an antique vault with equanimity! I think not, for however brave a man may be, it is the law of Nature that he should thrill with fear at the approach of the supernatural.

I sat smoking and thinking in the twilight, which was a bad preparation for the event, as twilight thoughts are invariably mournful, and my own dear dead ones seemed to throng in the dusky shadow of the room, reproaching me in voiceless grief for the intention I had of profaning the sanctity of the Tomb. To rid myself of these melancholy reflections, and banish from my brain the mute crowd of ghosts, I went out for a walk, intending to call at the Casa Angello, in order to ask after the Signorina Bianca.

Petronella told me that the poor child was much better, but exhausted by the shock she had sustained at the Palazzo Morone, and had fallen into a deep sleep which would do her more good than all the drugs of the doctor. The worthy domestic was very wrathful at me, and wanted to know what I had told her "piccola," but I put her off with some excuse, as I had no desire that she should know the events of that day. On taking my departure I gave Petronella a note for the Signorina, which contained only three words, "Wait and hope," with instructions that it was to be delivered to her when she woke up. Petronella, somewhat mollified by my assurance that all would be right, promised to fulfil this commission, and I returned to my hotel very contented with the present aspect of affairs.

On regaining my bedroom I lay down about eight o'clock, in order to get a little sleep, but the remedy was worse than the disease, for when my eyes were closed the phantoms of waking hours reappeared still more vividly to my inner senses. However, I fought against the dread which threatened to overwhelm me, and fell into a comparatively dreamless slumber, from which I awoke shortly after eleven. Rising from the bed upon which I had thrown myself half dressed, I hurriedly completed my toilette, and bathed my burning face in cold water. On my arrival in Milan, I had bought one of those picturesque Italian cloaks which one only sees in England on the operatic stage, and throwing this around me; I put on a soft black wide-awake, so that what with the mantle draped around me, and my naturally dark face, I looked very much like a native of Italy. Lighting a cigarette, I took my heavy stick, and thus prepared, went out to keep my appointment with Luigi Beltrami on the Ponte Aleardi.

To the hot day had succeeded the hot night, but a strong dry wind was blowing which drove the filmy clouds across the face of the haggard-looking moon. A few stars peeped out here and there through the frail woof, and the chill moonlight waxed and waned with the appearing and disappearing of the pale planet, almost lost amid the wild confluence of drifting clouds. A misty circle round the moon was prophetic of rain, and under this wild, wind-vexed sky lay the sleeping city, dark and sombre, with the rough blasts sweeping drearily down the lonely streets.

In spite of the heat, so eerie was the aspect of the night that I drew my cloak around me with a shiver of nervous fear, and leaving the Piazza Vittorio Emanuele, hastened along the Via Pallone, in the direction of the Ponte Aleardi. I arrived there just as the clock of St. Fermo sounded the three-quarters, and as Beltrami was not yet at the meeting place, I leaned on the balustrade of the bridge and watched the grey waters swirling under the fitful light of the moon. I could not help thinking of the strange events which had taken place since I had last occupied the same position—the antique chamber with its associations of love and crime—the Teatro Ezzelino, where I had beheld the phantom of Lucrezia Borgia—the grief and pain of poor little Bianca, and the extraordinary-conversation I had held with Beltrami a few hours before. It was all most unreal and feverish, this mediaeval intrigue into which I had been drawn; and I question if any student of singing had ever before been involved in such a bizarre adventure—an adventure which I hoped and prayed and trusted would end to-night.

A Creature of the Night

Buried in these sombre reflections I did not hear the sound of approaching footsteps, and it was only when I felt a hand on my shoulder that I turned round, with a sudden start, to see the Marchesa standing beside me wrapped in his military cloak, and accompanied by a man who waited a little way off in respectful silence.

"Bravo, Signor Hugo!" cried the Marchesa in a cheerful tone, "you have been waiting long?"

"About a quarter of an hour. So you have not obtained the key, Beltrami?"

"Unfortunately I have not! However, here is Matteo, and I daresay we shall manage to get the door open in some way. Come, Caro," continued Beltrami, taking my arm, "we have no time to lose. Ecco!"

I do not believe Beltrami had any nerves, for the whole way to the burial-ground he chatted cheerfully about the antidote, the Contessa and the tenor, not appearing to be at all impressed with the solemnity of the affair. What Matteo felt I do not know, as he never opened his mouth, but glided after us like a shadow, until we arrived at the broken wall.

The Marchesa climbed over first, his long sabre clashing heavily against the stones as he jumped down on the other side. I followed without delay, and Matteo, having joined us, we went on through the dense shade of the cypress trees, until we arrived at the forbidding-looking tomb, the sight of which put me in mind of my uncanny adventure.

Beltrami, undeterred by the flaming sword of the guardian angel, tried the iron door, on the chance that it might be unlocked; but finding it fast closed, signed to Matteo to get to work at once. Without a word the man obeyed, and as the moon was now shining down in her full splendour, he could see perfectly well, without the aid of artificial light, for, although he carried a torch, Beltrami did not wish it lighted, in case the glare should attract attention.

While Matteo was working away at the lock I took my seat on the fallen stone near the door, and Beltrami, throwing off his cloak, flung himself down on the grass beside me.

"Dio, how hot I am!" he exclaimed, wiping his brow.

"And how very imprudent, Luigi. Remember, you are in uniform."

"Ma foi, I'm never in anything else," retorted the Marchese gaily; "don't trouble yourself, Hugo, no one will dare to come near the cemetery, at this hour, so, uniform or no uniform, I'm safe from observation. Will you have a cigar?"

"No, thank you. But you surely do not intend to smoke now?"

"Why not?" said Beltrami, lighting his cigar; "it cannot harm the Signori Morone, and I've no wish to go down into that evil-smelling vault without taking some precaution against fever. Ecco!"

"Oh, well, do as you will," I replied, indifferently, beginning myself to grow callous; "but I want to ask you something, Luigi."

"Ebbene!"

"Was Count Giorgio Morone really mad?"

"Eh! I'm not sure. Every one said he was, but I did not think so. Dame! they call every man mad who has brains above his fellows, and Morone was a clever man. Though, to be sure, it was curious his hiding this poison in the vault, instead of destroying it altogether."

"That would certainly have been the wisest plan."

"Very likely, but you see, my wise Englishman, Morone had a tenderness for this child of his brain, and he could not bear to destroy his work. Oh! inventors are wonderful egotists, I assure you."

At this moment Matteo, who had been working in silence for some considerable time, approached his master.

"Eccellenza, it is open!"

"Bene!" cried Beltrami, springing to his feet, and wrapping his cloak around him again, "give me the torch. Come, Signor Hugo, let us go down, and you, Matteo, stay at the door, and see that we are not interrupted."

"Si, Eccellenza!"

Beltrami stepped cautiously into the tomb, and I followed him, then half closing the iron door so that the light might not attract attention, he fired the torch, the flame of which shot upward with a red flare and resinous odour of smoke, showing us that we stood on the top of a flight of steep steps which led downward into the darkness. A chill, humid atmosphere pervaded this abode of the dead, and seemed to penetrate into my very bones, notwithstanding the heavy cloak I wore.

For a moment we paused on the height, looking downward into the thick gloom; then Beltrami descended the steps slowly, tossing the flaring torch up and down, to and fro, in order to illuminate the darkness, and as I followed him the smoke, with its pungent odour, streamed backward towards my face. A bat, startled by the glare, flew round our heads with a rapid sweep of its noiseless wings, then vanished through the half-open door into the night beyond, like some escaping spectre of the tomb.

At last we reached the floor of the vault, which was paved with broad black marble slabs, so highly polished that the crimson blaze of the torch was reflected therein. All around in niches were innumerable coffins, some covered with tattered velvet palls, while others stood out grim and bare in their leaden hideousness, the coverings having long since mouldered away. In the gloom, there every no w and then could be perceived the glimmer of some white figure sculptured on the massive wall, the glitter of tarnished silver ornaments, and the outlines of painted devices, while the smoky torch with its angry flame cast strange gleams upon these mouldy splendours of the dead.

In the centre, on a square stone hidden by a rich pall of black velvet, embroidered with armorial devices in silver braid, rested the gorgeous coffin of the last Morone, which I presume was to remain there until the death of the Contessa, when it would be removed to its already-prepared niche to make way for the sole survivor of the proud race.

The Marchesa at once advanced to the coffin, and waving the torch above it, examined the decorations closely. True to his determination he was smoking, and it gave me an unpleasant shock to see this cloaked figure behaving so disrespectfully in the solemn presence of the dead.

"Bene!" he said at length in a satisfied tone, "there is one thing certain. It is not **in** the coffin!"

"How do you know that, Beltrami?"

"Because the lid is screwed down, and the Contessa, who as you say was alone, could not have taken that off. Besides, even if she did, Madame Morone knows the value of time too well to waste it in replacing the lid. No, it is not in the coffin, but it's somewhere about the coffin."

"What makes you think so, Luigi?"

"All this elaborate silver work! There's too much of it to be there without some reason. Caro, Hugo, just hold the torch and I will make an examination."

I took the torch in silence and watched his actions with great curiosity. The coffin, as he said, was most elaborately adorned with silver work representing the arms of the Morone family, interspersed with wreaths of flowers and tangled seaweed. On the lid was a broad silver plate similarly adorned, setting forth the name, titles, and date of death of the deceased, and round the oblong sides of this shell ran another broad wreath of flowers, shells, crests, and seaweeds, designed in the same style as the decorations on the lid. Beltrami, who was a clever prestidigitateur and could perform the most marvellous tricks with cards, had a wonderfully delicate sense of touch, and trusting to this more than to his eyes he ran his slender fingers rapidly over the raised silver ornaments on the lid of the coffin.

I saw at once that he suspected this useless silver ornamentation concealed some secret hiding-place in which the bottles of the poison and its antidote were hidden, and I could not help admiring the wonderful cleverness of the man in thinking of such an extraordinary idea, particularly as I saw at once that if the poison were anywhere it would be in some such ingenious hiding-place.

After running his hands twice or thrice over the lid, he shook his head with an angry ejaculation, and desisted from his apparently useless task.

"Dame! it's not on the top, that's certain," he said, stamping his foot with vexation. "My fingers never, deceive me, and I'm sure I haven't missed anything. From what I've told you I don't think it can be within the coffin. Ecco! let us try the sides."

He carefully wiped the tips of his fingers with his handkerchief, and beginning at the side nearest the head ran his fingers delicately along the cold silver work. Nothing was discoverable at the side, but when he came to the end of the coffin at the feet of the corpse he gave a cry of triumph which brought me at once to his side.

"Bravo, Hugo! what did I tell you! The poison-bottle was in the silver work. Behold, infidel, how truly I speak. Ecco!"

The decoration at this narrow end was a heart-shape shield, bearing the arms of the Morone family and wreathed with flowers, but this shield, which curved outward had a spring at the top. In touching this, the whole shield fell downward, working on a single hinge, and there was a cavity in which a small bottle might easily be concealed.

"I see the hiding-place, Beltrami; but where is the poison!"

"Eh! have you forgotten the visit of the Contessa, mon ami?"

"No, no! of course not! She, no doubt, took the poison away, and, I daresay, the antidote with it."

"Mon cher, I will never make anything of you," cried the Marchese in despair; "what did I tell you about that letter?"

"You said that no doubt as the Count was afraid of it being found by his wife he would only mention where the poison was concealed, and keep silent about the antidote."

"Ebbene! The Contessa knew nothing of the existence of the antidote, so when she found the poison she thought she had found all. Is that not so, you stupid Englishman?"

"Yes, I suppose so."

"Good! Well I, knowing of the existence of the antidote not mentioned in the letter, and only finding the poison at the feet, would naturally look for the antidote—where?"

"I daresay at the head," I suggested, after a pause; upon which Beltrami laughed, and walked to the other end of the coffin.

"Of course; it would be the most natural thing to do. Behold, mon ami!"

He touched the top of a similar shield at the head of the coffin; it fell stiffly outward, and lo! in the hollow of the curve, lay a small bottle, which Beltrami took in his hand, and then restored the shield to its former position.

"Luigi, you are a most wonderful man!" I cried, with a burst of genuine admiration at the clever way in which he had guessed this riddle.

"I only use my brains," he replied, with a gratified laugh. "The poison being at the feet, it was not difficult to guess the antidote was at the head; particularly as the decorations on both ends of the coffin are the same precisely. Dame! if the Contessa had only known the antidote was in existence she would have argued in the same way as I have done, and carried it off as she had done the poison."

"Well, we can now restore that unfortunate Pallanza to life."

"Yes, I suppose so," said the Marchese, slipping the bottle containing the antidote into his pocket; "though he certainly does not deserve to have another chance of existence. But as it is inconvenient keeping him in my house, I suppose I must send him away on his legs. Ecco! But come along, Hugo. We have what we desire, and I care not for this abode of death."

We went up the stairs and out of the iron door, where we found Matteo still keeping guard. It was quite a relief to get out of the fetid atmosphere of the tomb into the cool, fresh air again, and I felt like a released prisoner who was free for the first time after many years. The Marchese, however, man of iron as he was, did not seem to be affected in any way, but wrapping his cloak round him, prepared to go.

"Can you close that door again, Matteo?"

"Eccellenza! it is done!"

"Bene! Let us go!"

In fact the moment we emerged, Matteo, knowing our task was concluded, had reclosed the door by some trick known to himself; so we all three climbed over the broken wall, and took our way to the Ponte Aleardi.

"And when are you going to give Pallanza the antidote?" I asked, as we walked along arm-in-arm.

"Eh! Signor Hugo, to-morrow!"

"Why not to-night?"

"Ma foi! I am tired. A few hours will not make much difference; besides, I want a doctor to be present. The antidote will revive the poor devil, but he will be so weak after going without food all these days that the doctor will have to take charge of him."

"Well, then, I will see you to-morrow, Marchese. At what hour?"

"Two and a half in the afternoon. I attend to my military duties in the morning. Buona sera, Hugo!"

"Good-night, Beltrami."

We parted with a hearty shake of the hand, and I suppose after all I had gone through, nature was thoroughly tired out; for I went straight to bed and slept soundly without dreams, visions, or phantoms of any kind coming to disturb my rest.

✳✳✳

CHAPTER XIV

THE NEW LAZARUS

For the first time during the week I had a good night's rest, for ever since my adventure the events in connection therewith had succeeded one another so rapidly that my brain was kept in too active a state to admit of slumber, but now that everything seemed to be at an end, that the antidote had been found, and that Pallanza would be restored to Bianca Angello, my mind was relieved of the strain upon it, and I slept soundly till morning. In fact, I did not waken till nearly eleven o'clock, and having taken my bath I dressed myself slowly, made a good meal at midday, and altogether felt better than I had done for the last week.

As my appointment with Beltrami was for half-past two I did not go to Casa Angello for my usual singing lesson, not wishing to see the Signorina until I could tell her the good news that her lover was alive and well. It was true Beltrami had asserted that the antidote would awaken the young man from his death-like slumber, but remembering that he had now been in this state of catalepsy for nearly a week, I felt doubtful as to the success of the experiment. However, a few hours would now decide the fate of Pallanza for life or death, and in the event of the antidote acting according to the expectations of the Marchese, I promised myself I should be the first to carry the joyful news of this wonderful resurrection to the Signorina Bianca.

When two o'clock struck I could no longer restrain my impatience, but set off without further delay to see Beltrami at his apartments. He had just returned from the barracks, and was taking some biscuits and wine when I was announced, but jumped up when he saw me and came forward with outstretched hand,—

"Eh! mon ami, I am delighted to see you! Sit down, while I finish this small meal. Will you have a glass of wine?"

"No, thank you, Marchese!"

"Then take a cigarette, there are some on that table."

The Marchese returned to his wine and biscuits, while I lighted a cigarette, and lay down On the sofa.

"Excuse me lying down, Luigi, but our last night's experience has knocked me up terribly."

"You would never do for a soldier, Signor Hugo! I've been drilling some stupid recruits all the morning, and I feel perfectly fresh. Ecco! I'm glad to see you, however, as I have some news to tell you."

"About Pallanza?"

"Eh? No! About Madame Morone."

"Ah! she has found out we were at the vault?"

"Dame! not a bit of it. She left Verona by the five o'clock train last night."

"Left Verona!" I cried, rising hastily from my recumbent position. "Why has she gone away?"

"Eh! who knows?" replied Beltrami, shrugging his shoulders. "She didn't even leave a message for me, her promised husband. I think, myself, the empty pillar of yesterday startled her. She evidently thought everything was discovered, therefore has gone to Rome so that she Can appeal to the King in case of trouble."

"And what are you going to do, Marchese?"

"The best thing I can do under the circumstances. I have applied for, and obtained, leave of absence, so I will give this infernal tenor the antidote to-day, and start for Rome by the night train."

"But when you arrive at Rome?"

"I will see Madame Morone, and tell her that I removed the body of Pallanza from the pillar."

"The body, Beltrami! You forget Pallanza is alive!"

"Of course he is, but I'm not going to tell her that. Cospetto! if she discovered that this devil of a tenor was still in existence my power over her would be gone, and she would not marry me. Ecco!"

"But as Pallanza will sing again, she is bound to find it out sooner or later."

"Eh! no doubt, Signor Hugo; but by the time she finds out I hope to be married. In that case it does not matter. Besides, I am going to make Pallanza promise not to sing anywhere for a month."

"Suppose he refuses?"

"He won't refuse. Dame! he owes me something for bringing him into existence again."

"And what about the doctor?"

"He will soon be here," said Beltrami, glancing at his watch; "I expect him every minute."

"Will he keep this affair quiet?"

"Per Bacco! I should think so, mon ami. I ascertained that before I told him anything. Not that I told him much, ma foi, no! I invented a delightful story about Pallanza, which he swallowed as easily as I do this wine."

"And the story?"

"I have not the time to tell it to you, but it is a beautiful story, worthy of Boccaccio. Oh, he will keep his mouth shut, I promise you, Hugo. He is a great friend of mine, and I never associate with those who talk of other people's business."

"Have you the antidote, Marchese?"

"Here it is," said Beltrami, rising and taking the small bottle from his desk near the window; "and, ma foi! here is the doctor coming up the street."

"How fond you are of French," I remarked, laughingly. "Parisian ejaculations are never out of your mouth."

                                        A Creature of the Night

"One must ejaculate in some language, Hugo, and I've been so often in Paris that I've got into the trick in some way."

"What about London?"

"Your city of fogs! Eh! You know I cannot master your tongue, Signor Hugo. 'You are a beautiful mees; I loove you'—Dio! what a difficulty I had in learning those two sentences."

"Which are perfectly useless."

"I have not found them so. But here is Signor Avenza, the doctor I spoke of. Good-day, for the second time, my friend. Permit me to introduce Signor Hugo Cranston, an Englishman."

The doctor, a fat little man with a round smiling face and two twinkling black eyes, executed an elaborate bow, for which purpose he brought his feet smartly together in military fashion, and, having thus saluted me, rashly entered into a contest with the English language, which vanquished him at once.

"I spik Inglis," he said, mincingly. Then, with a gigantic effort, "Gif me your tongue! Ah! he is bad. Dis writing is your cure. Goot-day! I vil taake a leetle valk wis you agin."

Signor Avenza had evidently learned these choice English phrases for the purposes of his profession.

While this lesson in philology was going on the Marchese had opened the door leading into the room where Pallanza was concealed, and called to us to enter. Both the doctor and myself, obeying the summons, went through the bedroom, and soon found ourselves by the couch, whereon lay the still form of the young man, with that terrible death-in-life look on his white face.

"See, Avenza, this is what I spoke about," said Beltrami, holding up a small phial filled with a red liquid. "It is the antidote to the poison which this Pallanza was foolish enough to take."

"And all through a love disappointment," replied Avenza, lifting his eyes. "Ah! the poor young man!"

I now began to see the kind of story Beltrami had told Avenza to account for the condition of Pallanza, and I must say it did credit to his powers of invention.

"The amount of the poison he took was ten drops." went on Beltrami, uncorking the bottle, "so it will require ten drops of this antidote to revive him, but when the life is once more in him I suppose he will be weak."

"Most certainly," answered Avenza, nodding his head, "since you say he has been like this for nearly a week. But proceed, Marchese, I am anxious to see the result of this antidote."

Beltrami bent over the face of the unconscious man, and forced the teeth slightly apart with a spoon he held in his left hand. Having done this, he poised the bottle over the pale lips, and began to pour the red liquid drop by drop into the mouth.

Both Avenza and myself bent forward eagerly to watch the operation, and held our breaths with anxiety as the Marchese counted, slowly,—

"One, two, three, four, five, six, seven, eight, nine, ten!"

The body made no movement, and Beltrami drew back, looking somewhat anxious.

"Dio! I am afraid ten drops are not enough!"

"Wait," said Avenza, taking his watch out of his pocket, and placing his fingers on the pulse of the seemingly-dead man. "You cannot expect this antidote to act at once."

The minutes passed slowly, and we all three remained with our eyes eagerly watching for some sign of life on that still face, while Avenza occasionally glanced at his chronometer.

"His pulse beats," he said at length in a low voice, "faintly, it is true, but still it beats."

I heaved a sigh of relief, but Beltrami remained silently looking at the face of Pallanza with an anxious frown.

"She cannot have given him fifteen," he muttered under his breath, "if So, he would have been dead by this time; but his pulse beats, so he is alive."

He looked irresolutely at the phial in his hand, and then turned to Avenza, who Was still counting the feeble pulsation of the blood.

"Doctor, I will give him three more drops!"

"Eh! and why not?" replied Avenza, raising his eye-brows; "as that is an antidote a few drops more or less cannot kill him after the dose of poison he has taken."

The Marchese made no further remark, but, bending forward again, he held the phial over the half-open mouth for the second time.

"One, two, three!"

This time the effect was magical; for after an interval of about two or three minutes, we saw a shudder run through the rigid body, the left arm jerked upward in a spasmodic manner, the face flushed crimson with the rush of blood once more flowing freely through the arteries, and at last the heavy eyelids lifted slowly. Pallanza gazed at us with a dazed, unseeing expression, then some tremendous force seemed to take possession of the body, for a spasm of pain passed over his face, a choking cry issued from his lips, and in a moment he was shrieking, writhing, twisting, rolling and plunging about the bed like a demoniac. All the nerves and muscles which had been dead and inert for so many days were now waking again to life, and the agony which racked his frame from head to foot must have been truly terrible. Both Beltrami and myself made a step forward to hold down this agonized body, but Avenza stopped us.

"The antidote is doing its work," he said rapidly; "the dead body is renewing its life throughout every particle. Wait! wait! the paroxysm will soon pass away."

The doctor was right, for in a short time the writhing stopped, the cries grew fainter, and at last, with a heavy sigh, the young man sank back on the pillows in a state of exhaustion, on seeing which, both

Beltrami and the doctor ran out of the room to get some brandy, leaving me alone with this new Lazarus. During their absence he opened his eyes, to which the light of sanity had now returned, and spoke in a feeble voice,—

"Where am I?"

"With friends."

"And the Contessa?"

"She is not here! You are quite safe! Hush! do not speak, I beg of you."

Pallanza gave me a look of gratitude, then, closing his eyes, relapsed into silence. Avenza returned with a glass of weak brandy and water, which he gave to the young man in spoonfuls, 'while I went back into the sitting-room to see Beltrami, whom I found standing by the window with a frown on his face.

"Ebbene?" he asked, turning round.

"He is much better, and I think will soon be all right."

"That's a blessing. But what a nuisance! I want to go to Rome to-night by the five o'clock train, but Avenza tells me that Pallanza will have to sleep for a few hours, so I won't have an opportunity of speaking to him."

"Go with a light heart, my dear Beltrami; I will arrange everything."

"You will?"

"Yes; Pallanza can sleep in that room for an hour or two, then I will get a fiacre and take him to his lodgings. No one shall come near him but myself, and when he is quite sensible I will make him promise all you want."

"Bene! you are a good friend, my dear Hugo," said the Marchese, in a tone of relief; "but do you think he will do what you ask?"

"Most certainly! I can force him to obey me."

"How so?"

"By threatening to tell Signorina Angello about his affair with Madame Morone. She knows nothing as yet, and Pallanza is afraid of

A Creature of the Night

her knowing. Witness the lie he told about that note at the Ezzelino, asking him to come to the Palazzo!"

Beltrami, with his cynical estimate of the Contessa's character, was not at all disturbed by this somewhat blunt speech, but laughed cheerfully.

"Eh! Hugo. I think I will make you. Italian after all. Your plan is a good one, mon ami, so make Pallanza promise not to sing anywhere for a month, to leave Verona and keep quiet. By that time I will be married to the Contessa, and all will be well."

"I will arrange everything as you desire, Luigi."

"Excellent! Then that trouble is off my mind."

At this moment the doctor entered, rubbing his fat hands together with an expression of glee.

"Eh, he sleeps, this young man," he said in a satisfied tone, "he will sleep for one, two, three hours, then, if you like, Marchese, you can send him to his own house."

"Signor Hugo will attend to all that, Avenza."

"Bene! Well, Marchese, à revederci! And you, Signor."

"Wait a moment, Signor Avenza; I am coming too."

"Where are you going! Hugo?" asked Beltrami, looking at me in some surprise, and nodding his head in the direction of Pallanza. I crossed over to him, and while Avenza was getting his hat, whispered in his ear,—

"I am going to the Ezzelino to find out Pallanza's address, so as to know where to take him."

"Ah! a good idea! I will wait here till you return."

I accompanied Signor Avenza to the Piazza Vittorio Emanuele, where we parted. I then went to the Teatro Ezzelino and found out Pallanza's address from the stage-door keeper. While I was returning to Beltrami's rooms I saw Peppino, and arranged with him to be at the Via Cartoni at seven o'clock that evening to take a sick gentleman away. At first Peppino objected, being, like all Italians, terribly afraid of disease, but I soon quieted his objections, and he promised to call as directed.

On returning to Beltrami I found him packing up, and at five o'clock he took his departure for Rome, promising to write me immediately he arrived, and in return I assured him I would let him know everything as soon as I arranged matters with Pallanza.

That young man slept until nearly seven, when he woke up and began to ask me questions as to where he was. I insisted upon his keeping quiet, telling him I was a doctor, and when Peppino arrived with his fiacre I wrapped him up in his cloak so as to hide his stage costume, and helped him downstairs to the carriage. We soon arrived at his lodgings, where, dismissing Peppino, I made Pallanza go to bed at once, and gave him a light supper, together with some weak brandy and water. After this he fell asleep, and I sat watching by his bed all night, wondering why I was such a fool as to do all this for a cynical man of the world like Beltrami, who would probably laugh at my good nature when all was over. Yet there was something about Luigi Beltrami which I liked; and in spite of his affected cynicism and his extraordinarily loose notions of right and wrong, I believe that he had a sincere regard for me, which regard I considered not the least curious part of his whimsical nature, seeing that my character was the antithesis of his own in every way. Perhaps it was by the law of contrast, or illustrated inversely the saying that "like draws to like;" but whatever was the reason, though we had nothing in common either in nationality or character, yet we were friends, and I leave this problem to be worked out by those who deny that such an enigma can exist.

****

A Creature of the Night

CHAPTER XV

FOUND

Guiseppe Pallanza slept soundly all night, while I took snatches of sleep in the armchair by his bedside. At nine o'clock in the morning he awoke, feeling much stronger, and after I had given him something to eat I prepared to go out.

"Where are you going, Signor?" asked Pallanza in an anxious tone.

"I am going to send a doctor to see you, and then I am going to the Casa Angello."

"And for what reason?"

"To bring Signorina Bianca here!"

"Do you know the Signorina Bianca?"

"Very well, Signor Pallanza. I am the Englishman of whom you have no doubt heard her speak."

"Signor Hugo! yes, I know," muttered Guiseppe; and then, after a pause, "I wish to speak to you, I wish to tell you something."

"You shall tell me all shortly, but meanwhile lie down quietly, and when the doctor comes say nothing about the Palazzo Morone."

"Ah!" cried Pallanza, starting up in his bed, "do you know that horrible place?"

"I know all! But there, you are still weak," I answered, forcing him to lie down. "When I return I will speak to you about some important matters."

"Important!—to me?"

"Yes, and to the Contessa Morone."

"Ah! that terrible woman."

"Meanwhile, Signor Pallanza, say nothing about your visit to the palace or about Madame Morone."

"Not a word! And you will bring Bianca to see me?"

"Yes! I promise you."

With this hope, Pallanza was perfectly contented, and after instructing his landlady, who was in a state of great bewilderment at this sudden reappearance, to look after him, I went out to find Avenza. Fortunately he was well known in Verona, and I had no difficulty in discovering his house. He saw me at once, listened to my account of the way Pallanza had passed the night, and promised to see him without delay. Having thus carried out satisfactorily the first part of my mission, I departed to perform the second, which involved a somewhat embarrassing interview with Signorina Angello.

On arriving at the house of the Maestro, I was received by Petronella, who threw up her hands with an appeal to the saints when she saw my haggard appearance and burst out into a volley of questions.

"Eh! Signor Inglese. Is it not well with you? San Pietro! how the wine does change a face. Here has the Maestro been asking for you every day! 'Well! Well!' said I, 'he has gone away like the lover of the piccola!' And it is true! I see how you return. Eh! Madonna, all men are bad. I have been married—I know."

"You are wrong on this occasion, Petronella. I have not been at the wine, as you seem to think!"

"But your face, Signor Inglese—like that of a sick person! Gran dio!"

"Comes from sitting up all night by the bedside of Guiseppe Pallanza."

Petronella clapped her hands together with an ejaculation of delight

"He is found, then, the poor young man! Ah! it is well I did not waste a centesimo in masses; and those priests are such thieves. Eh!

　　　　　　　　　　　　　　　A Creature of the Night

this news will be like wine to the piccola. Go in! go in, Signor Inglese! the Signorina is there, but the Maestro! he is in bed, which is the best place for him, say I."

After this breathless harangue Petronella ushered me into the sitting-room, where I found Bianca sitting by the window, contemplating a portrait of her lost lover. She arose when she saw me and came forward with an anxious look on her paleface, while the faithful but noisy domestic left the apartment.

"Well, Signorina, do you feel better?"

"Yes, yes, Signore, much better; but you have news!—news of Guiseppe."

"The best of news, my poor child. Guiseppe is found, and is now at his lodgings."

The blood rushed into her hitherto pale cheeks, her melancholy dark eyes sparkled with joy, and from a pallid, worn-looking girl she changed into a bright, joyful woman. It was a most wonderful transformation, as if a wan lily had suddenly blossomed under the wand of some fairy into a rich red rose.

"Signor Hugo! Signor Hugo! Ah, the good news! Oh, how happy I am! He is alive, then? he is well! Oh, say he is well, Signor Hugo!"

"Signorina, he is still weak after his adventure, and at present he is in bed."

"Oh, let me go to him! let me go at once! He may die, my poor Guiseppe!"

"No he will not die; but put on your hat and I will take you to him, for you alone, Signorina, can nurse him back to health and strength."

Bianca ran to put on her hat and tell the Maestro the good news, which evidently delighted the old man greatly, judging from the extraordinary chuckling sounds which shortly proceeded from his bedroom. Petronella at the doorway celebrated a noisy triumph on her own account, and at last amid the chucklings of the patriarch and the loud delight of his handmaiden, Bianca took her departure under my wing to visit the newly-found prodigal.

She absolutely danced along the pavement, so exuberant was her delight at the good news, and I thought how easily I could damp this joy by telling her the true story of Guiseppe's disappearance. It was a cruel thought, and I regretted it the moment after it flashed across my mind; for it would have been the wanton act of a boy crushing a butterfly to have destroyed the happy ignorance of this merry child, who, tripping gaily along by my side, put me in mind of the smiling Hebe of the Greeks, that charming incarnation of joyous maidenhood.

"Signore!" said Bianca, moderating her transports, "you have not told me the reason of Guiseppe's absence."

"I am afraid there is very little to tell, Signorina! He was lured to the Palazzo by an enemy, who kept him there until last night, when, luckily, I discovered where he was concealed and released him."

"Ah, Signor Hugo, how can I thank you for your kindness! Then my poor Guiseppe was hidden in that terrible room?"

"He was concealed near it, at all events," I replied evasively.

"And the voice in the darkness, Signor? Oh, that cruel, cruel voice! It. has haunted my dreams ever since!"

"It was nothing, Signorina; it was—it was a friend of mine, who came to assist me to look for Guiseppe!"

"Was it a signor or a Signora?" asked Bianca, who, evidently in her nervous agitation, had not distinguished the feminine tones of the unknown.

"It was a signor! a young signor whom I know!"

"But he saw us in the darkness. Dio! how terrible."

"No; he did not see us. He guessed we were there, as I told him we were going to look for Guiseppe, and he came to assist me."

Bianca was satisfied with this—I flatter myself—skilful explanation, and stopped asking questions, much to my relief. The number of lies

I was forced to tell in connection with this affair was truly surprising, but as it was absolutely necessary to keep this poor child in ignorance of the true state of the case, I ventured to hope that the Recording Angel would treat them in the same way as he did the oath of my Uncle Toby, in Sterne's delightful story. Italian intrigue, from the experience I had of it, was certainly very little to my taste, as I was by no means a convert to the Jesuitical maxim that the end justifies the means, therefore it was with a thankful heart that I saw the whole intricate affair was nearly finished.

By this time we had arrived at Pallanza's lodgings, and I placed Bianca in an outer room with strict injunctions that she was not to leave it until I called her.

"Guiseppe is still weak, Signorina, and I must prepare him for your coming."

The fact is I wanted to carry out my promise to Beltrami, in asking Pallanza to live in retirement for a few months, and, until this was arranged, I was unwilling that he should see Bianca. The poor child fully believing what I said, promised to obey me faithfully in all things; so leaving her in the outer room I went in to see Pallanza, whom I found eagerly expecting my arrival.

To my surprise, the young man was up and dressed, as Dr. Avenza, finding him So much better, had insisted on him leaving his bed, to remain in which, he declared, was weakening; so I found Pallanza walking slowly to and fro to exercise his muscles, but on seeing me he came forward With an anxious look,—

"Is she here, Signor Hugo? Has Bianca come?"

"She is in the next room, Signor! No, do not go to her. I wish to speak to you."

"I am at your service, Signor Hugo. You have done so much for me that I can never repay you."

"Yes, you can by telling me how you went to the Palazzo Morone on that night."

"I will tell all, Signore! You have a right to know. But, Bianca?"

"She knows nothing."

A look of relief came over the anxious face of the young man, and we both sat down to continue the conversation.

"I met Madame Morone at Rome, Signore," said Pallanza with some faint hesitation, "and we were together a great deal. I did not love her exactly, but she being a great lady flattered my pride. Of course, I should have remembered Bianca, but she was not beside me, and as to the Contessa! ah, Signore Hugo, who can escape when a woman wills? Madame Morone made me afraid at last. She is a tigress, that woman, and threatened to kill me if I left her for another. I saw how dangerous was her love, and telling her I was going to marry the Signorina Angello, left Rome for Verona. She followed me here and took me to the Palazzo Morone on Sunday, where she exhausted every means of making me give up Bianca. I should not tell you all this about a woman, Signor, but by her attempt to kill me she has released me from the laws of honour. Cospetto! she is a mistress of the devil. Her rage is terrible, and on Sunday she implored, she wept, she raged, she threatened, but I was true to Bianca, and at last escaped from the palazzo intending never to see her again. On Monday night, however, I received a letter——"

"From a dying friend?" I interrupted meaningly.

"Eh! I said so in order to keep the affair from Bianca, as I knew if she heard about it I should be lost. No! Signor Hugo. The letter was from the Contessa, saying that if I did not come by eleven o'clock to the room in the palazzo, in order to bid her farewell, she would go at once to the Signorina Angello and tell all. Per Bacco! Signor, you may guess my fear at this message; and I determined to go to the palazzo at any cost. The opera was long that night, and before the curtain descended it was past eleven. I was so afraid of the Contessa fulfilling her threat that I did not wait to change my costume, but throwing on my cloak over my dress of Faust, went at once to the palazzo. She was not in the room, and I had a horrible fear that I was too late, but I waited for some time, and she came. We had another scene of tears, reproaches and rage, then——"

A Creature of the Night

"I can tell you the rest, Signor Pallanza. She gave you the poison in a cup of wine, and when you fell at her feet she shut you up in a hiding-place, from whence you were rescued."

"By you, Signor, by you?"

"No; by the Marchese Beltrami, who took you to his house, and after many days revived you with an antidote to the poison which he obtained with great difficulty."

"But the Marchese! You, Signor, how did you see all this?"

"Ah! that is a long story. I will tell it to you another time, but at present you must promise me something."

"Anything, Signor Hugo! For you have saved my life from that terrible woman."

"She is indeed a terrible woman! and it is to escape her vengeance that I advise you not to sing for at least two months."

"But my engagement at the Ezzelino?"

"Pay forfeit-money. Say you are ill and cannot sing. Then return to Milan with the Signorina and marry her at once."

"But the Contessa?"

"Has gone to Rome for the present; but as soon as she finds out you are alive she will come after you; so, if you are wise, Signor Pallanza, you will obtain some engagement out of Italy."

"Basta, Signor! your advice is good, and I will do what you ask. For two months I will not sing. I will pay the forfeit-money to the Ezzelino and return to Milan with Bianca. It is best so. Per Bacco! what a demon I have escaped!"

I felt greatly relieved that everything had thus been settled, so arose from my chair to take Pallanza to the Signorina, after which I intended to go straight to my hotel and write a letter to Beltrami, telling him of all that had taken place.

"Come, Signor Pallanza, lean on me, and I will take you to Bianca."

"Ah! cara Bianca," he cried joyfully, as I led him to the door; "Bianca, Bianca, gioja della mia vita!"

"Guiseppe!"

She saw him standing with outstretched arms on the threshold of the room, and with a cry of joy flew towards him like a bird to its nest, and flung herself on his breast.

As for me, I went out of the room and left them together.

∗∗∗

CHAPTER XVI

AN INTERRUPTED HONEYMOON

Well, at last I was back in Milan, much to my satisfaction, as after the strange adventures I had met with in Verona that city became positively hateful to me. Two months had elapsed since the affair of the Palazzo Morone had come to an end, and during that time two marriages in connection therewith had been celebrated—that of Beltrami with the Contessa Morone, at Rome; and that of Guiseppe Pallanza with Signorina Bianca, at Milan. True to his promise, Guiseppe had forfeited his engagement at the Ezzelino, much to the wrath of the impresario, and had rested quietly since at Milan, passing most of his time with Bianca, who was now in a state of high glee preparing for her marriage.

It took place at the church of St. Stefano, in Milan, and out of consideration for the great age of the Maestro it was a very quiet affair, I being the only one present beyond the Angello household, but that was at the urgent request of both Bianca and her husband, who never forgot the services I had rendered them at Verona.

Thanks to my dexterity, Bianca never discovered the truth, and fully believed that Guiseppe had been kept a prisoner at the Palazzo Morone by some enemy who had lured him thither, by means of the letter purporting to come from a dying friend. At first, considering the weak way in which Guiseppe had acted, I did not consider that he deserved his good fortune in marrying such a charming girl as the Signorina, but during the time that preceded the marriage he was so devoted to her in every way, and apparently so remorseful for his amorous folly, that I quite forgave him his momentary infidelity. It was a very pretty wedding, the bride and bridegroom making a handsome couple, and when the ceremony was ended Signor and Signora Pallanza went to spend the honeymoon of a few days at Monza, and I was left alone in Milan.

Guiseppe had obtained an engagement at the Madrid Opera House, and on their return from Monza the young couple were to start almost immediately for Spain, leaving the Maestro under the tender care of Petronella. The old man's health had been failing sadly of late, and I doubted very much whether Bianca would find him alive on her return to Italy, seeing how frail he was in every respect.

Now that he was deprived of his right hand by the marriage of his granddaughter, the Maestro decided to give up teaching, at which decision I was profoundly sorry, as only having been with him a year I had still many things to learn in the art of vocalisation. There was, unfortunately, no one else with whom I could study the same system, for Paolo Angello taught the old, pure Italian method, of which he was the last exponent; and I infinitely preferred the round sonorous notes which his training produced to the shouting, colourless style of present-day singing, which curses the voice with a perpetual tremolo. The elaborate fioriture school of Pasta, Grisi, Ronconi, and Malibran has almost entirely passed away, and in its place what have we in Italy?—nothing but the present abominable fortissimo singing, without grace, sweetness, steadiness, or colour. The old Italian operas were composed not so much as stage performances as to show off the beauty, execution and brilliancy of the voice, while this new school of music-drama; designed principally for dramatic effect, is interpreted by singers who rely but little on the perfection of the vocal organ, and pride themselves not so much on the individual colouring of a single number as on the general broad effect of the whole. Fortunately, however, by incessant work during my one year under Angello, I had acquired a pretty good idea of his system of vocalisation, and hoped, by cautious industry in following out his hard and fast rules, to perfect my singing in accordance with his severely pure method.

Of the Marchese Beltrami and his wife I heard but little, save through the medium of the papers, as except one letter announcing his marriage with the Contessa, and thanking me for my attention to his interests, this ungrateful Luigi had not written to me. I consoled myself with philosophical reflections on the hollowness of friendship, when one day, towards the end of July, I was astonished to receive a visit from the Marchese.

Pallanza and his wife had returned to Milan, and were making preparations for their departure, which was now near at hand. I had just come back from a visit to the Maestro with whom they were staying, and was writing letters in my bedroom, when Beltrami's card was brought to me, upon which I ordered him to be shown into the room in which I was scribbling, so as to secure perfect privacy during our conversation.

In those days of poverty I lived like a cat on the tiles, up four flights of stairs just under the roof, and my one room served me for everything,— that is, as dining-room, reception-salon, and sleeping chamber. I took my meals at a sufficiently good restaurant near at hand, but otherwise the whole of my indoor life was bounded by the four walls of that small apartment, which contained an ingenious bed made to look like a sofa during the day, a wardrobe, a wash-stand, and a diminutive piano of German manufacture hired by myself. Yet, as Beranger sings, "One is happy in a garret at twenty years of age," and I think the days spent in that dingy Milanese eyry were among the most delightful of my life. I was young, enthusiastic, not badly off for a poor man, and devoted to my art, so I used to strum chords on that small piano while I practised my voice, act operatic scenes in front of the looking glass, and dream impossible dreams of applausive multitudes, of recklessly-generous impresarios, and of a career like that of the kings of song.

Then I had a view—a delightful view—of the red-roofed houses of Milan, seen from the window, with here and there a tall factory chimney, the slender tower of a church from whence sounded the jangling bells which used to irritate me, at least, every quarter of an hour, and just a glimpse of the white miracle of the great Duomo, rising like a fairy creation of milky lacework against the deeply blue sky. Even a vision of green trees I obtained by craning my head round the corner of the window, and when it was fine weather I looked at my roof-top view while enjoying a pipe, but when it rained—oh! heavens,

Milan was as dreary as London in a fog, and the blue skies of Italy became a fable of inventive minds. The intense heat changed to humid cold, and then I used to shut out this deceptive city of the Visconti by closing my window, and, retreating to the piano, practise exercises with a voice rendered, I am afraid, rather gruff by the chill terra-cotta floor and the damp atmosphere.

It was in this poor but honest abode, as the novelists say, that I received Beltrami, who entered gaily in civilian dress with outstretched hands, looking exactly the same as when I had last seen him at Verona. Marriage evidently had not changed him, as he had the same subtle smile on his dark face, talked in the same vein of cynicism, and interlarded his conversation with his usual number of French ejaculations.

"Eh! Hugo, mon ami," shaking both my hands heartily, "you are astonished to see me!"

"Considering you have never written me a line since your marriage, Beltrami, I certainly am."

I suppose I spoke with a certain bitterness, for the Marchese shrugged his shoulders, with a slight flush reddening his cheeks, and sat down on the bed—I mean, seeing it was daytime—the sofa.

"Ma foi! I am a newly-married man, Hugo!" he said, in an apologetic tone, "I have forgotten everything in the delightful society of that dear Contessa. But you are right to reproach me; I ought to have written, only I am so terribly negligent."

"And fickle; don't forget that trait of your character, Luigi. However, I'm glad to see you, fickle friend as you are."

"Dame! you don't spare me. I have called on you for a purpose!"

"That goes without saying. When one requires a friend one always knows where to find him. Well, Marchese, and in what way can I assist you?"

"I will tell you! but I see you do not ask after my wife?"

"I trust Madame Beltrami is well!" I said stiffly, not feeling any particularly warm feeling towards that lady.

                                    A Creature of the Night

"Yes! her health is good."

"And you are happy, Beltrami?"

"Tolerably! But tell me, how is Pallanza and his wife?"

"Oh, they live in Elysium, Marchese. At present they are in Milan, but leave next week for Madrid, where Pallanza is going to sing."

"He'll have to go by himself, then!"

"What do you mean?"

"That Madame, my very good wife, is hunting through Milan for his Elysium, with that famous bottle of poison in her pocket."

"Great heavens! Is she going to try and poison Pallanza again?"

"No! you remember the Latin maxim, 'Non bis in idem.' She is going to try the effect of the poison on his wife."

"And yet you can sit there calmly without making an attempt to save this innocent creature! Beltrami, it is infamous!"

I was walking up and down the room in a state of great excitement, for it seemed horrible and incomprehensible to see the Marchese sitting there so calm and composed, when he knew that a reckless, dangerous woman like his wife was in Milan bent on murder.

"Eh! Hugo, keep cool," said Beltrami, quietly. "It is just this affair I have come to see you about. Sit down, mon ami, and I'll tell you all about it."

"But every moment is of value!"

"No doubt, but as it will take madame some time to find out where Signor Pallanza is staying, I think we can safely talk for five minutes."

"Go on, then! I am all impatience!"

"So I see! Ebbene! When I went to Rome I told the Contessa that I had taken away Pallanza's body; but of course I did not say he was alive, and swore that if she did not marry me I would tell everything to the authorities. The sequel you know—she married me."

"A horrible contract," I muttered savagely, looking at the whole affair from an English point of view.

"I-think we argued that matter before," said Beltrami, coolly, "and, if I remember rightly, you did not agree with my reasons. However, it is too late now to blame me, seeing I have been married for nearly five weeks. We spent our honeymoon at Como—in fact, mon ami, we are spending it there still, only a perusal of yesterday's Lombardia sent my excellent wife off to this city in search of Signora Pallanza."

"I do not understand."

"No? Then I will enlighten you. Madame, my wife, thought this devil of a tenor dead, and, as he has been keeping quiet all this time, she never for a moment suspected the truth. I saw an announcement of his marriage in the newspapers, but you may be sure I did not let the Marchesa see it. Everything was going beautifully, and we were a model couple—outwardly—when, as ill-luck would have it, this paragraph appeared in the paper."

Beltrami handed me a copy of La Lombardia, and pointed to a paragraph, which I read. It stated that Guiseppe Pallanza, the famous tenor, was going to sing at the Grand Opera House, Madrid, and would be accompanied to Spain by his wife, the granddaughter of Maestro Angello, the celebrated teacher of singing.

"You can guess what a rage she was in," said Beltrami, when I had finished reading this fatal information. "Diavolo! she has a temper; but, as I told you, I am quite a match for Madame, and held my own during this furious quarrel. She demanded an explanation, and I gave her one."

"What? you told her——"

"Everything, mon ami. Your story, my story, Pallanza's story—all about the antidote, the vault, the supper. Eh! Hugo, she now knows as much as you or I. Mon Dieu, you should have seen her when I had finished!"

"Why? what did she do?"

"She smiled, that was all; but it was the smile that alarmed me."

"For your own safety?"

"Ma foi, no! I told her she need not try the poison on me, as I had the antidote. In reply, she gave one of those wicked laughs that freeze your blood, and said that Signora Pallanza had not an antidote, and it would be the worse for her."

"Then she intends to poison the poor girl?"

"I fancied so yesterday, and I was sure of it this morning, when I heard from my servants that the Marchesa Beltrami had gone to Milan. I knew what she was after, so followed by the next train, and came straight to you."

"And what do you want me to do, Beltrami?"

"Come with me at once to the Casa Angello, to warn Signora Pallanza! I suppose she is still staying with the Maestro Angello?"

"Yes, until she goes to Spain with her husband. Let us go at once, Luigi. But, oh! Beltrami, if we are too late!"

"Do not be alarmed! I have the antidote in my pocket."

***

CHAPTER XVII

NEMESIS

The Maestro had a very comfortable suite of apartments in Milan overlooking the Via Carlo Alberto, near the Piazza del Duomo, which were chosen by him on account of their situation, as he could sit at the window of his bedroom and amuse himself by gazing at the crowded street. This watching of the populace was his great delight, and when not giving a lesson he was generally stationed at his window, or else employed in reading **Il Seccolo**, which he did in a curious fashion, by holding it close to his best-seeing eye.

Of course, like all the entrances to these Milanese flats, the stairs were singularly damp, dark, and malodorous, and after running the gauntlet of a fat **portanaia**, who was devouring a large dish of polenta in her glass house, we climbed up the humid steps, and speedily arrived at the second storey, where dwelt the Maestro when in Milan. To make up for the filth under our feet the ceilings over our heads were gorgeously painted with mythological figures; and even at that moment I could not help recalling George Sands' remark anent the contrast between these two. However, we had no time to admire the clumsy Jupiter throwing fire-brand thunderbolts, for at this moment Petronella, who had seen us through the dingy glass of her own little sanctum, opened the door, and was about to burst into a torrent of greetings, when I stopped her to ask if the Signora Pallanza was at home.

"Yes! yes! the Signora is in, but she is engaged— engaged in talking with a lady—Dio! a great lady!

"Great heavens! we may be too late!" I muttered to Beltrami, who nodded his head silently. "Petronella, speak low. This gentleman and myself came on an important errand to the Signora. What is the lady's name?"

"Signor, she said she was the Marchesa Beltrami," replied Petronella, her jolly face growing rather grave at all this mystery.

"Is Signor Pallanza in?"

"No, Signor Hugo; he has gone to see an impresario."

"She is alone with Madame, let us go in at once," whispered Beltrami, exhibiting the first signs of alarm I had ever beheld in him.

"One moment! What about the Maestro, Petronella?"

"In his bedroom, Signor Hugo, at the window. Holy Saints! what is wrong?"

"Nothing! nothing! I will explain all shortly; but meanwhile, Petronella, show us a place where we can see into the room where the Signora is talking to the Marchesa, without being seen."

Beltrami nodded his head approvingly, for he saw my plan was to overhear the conversation, and only interrupt it should there be any danger to the Signora. Petronella was bursting with curiosity, but seeing, from the expression of our faces, that something important was going on, she screwed up her mouth with a shrewd look, to assure us we could depend upon her, and, closing the outside door cautiously, led us into the room adjacent to that in which the conversation was taking place. Pointing to an archway, veiled by curtains, to intimate that there was nothing else but the drapery to impede our hearing, she retired on tiptoe, with a puzzled, serious look on her usually merry face.

It seemed my fate to overhear mysterious conversations through veiled archways, but this one was not used as an entrance between the two rooms, for, as I peered through the curtains, 1 saw in front of them a small square table, upon which was placed a lacquered tray with glasses, and an oval straw-covered bottle of Chianti wine. I drew back for a moment, to see if Beltrami had noticed this obstacle to our sudden entrance into the room; but, instead of appearing dismayed, he had a grim, satisfied smile on his lips, as if he rather approved than otherwise of this table blocking up the doorway. Puzzled at this, I withdrew my eyes from his face, and looked again into the room beyond, where the Marchesa Beltrami was seated, talking to Bianca in what appeared to be a very friendly fashion.

It must be remembered that Bianca knew nothing about the Contessa Morone's intrigue with her husband, as both Guiseppe and myself had carefully kept all knowledge of the affair from her; and moreover, owing to her nervous agitation, she had not recognized the voice of the Marchesa when she spoke to us in the darkness of that fatal chamber at Verona. Consequently she was completely in ignorance of the real character of her visitor, and only beheld in her a lady who had called to see Signor Pallanza about some important business; this, as I afterwards learned, being the excuse she gave for her presence in the Casa Angello. It was truly terrible to see these two women seated together in friendly discourse, the one so innocent of the danger she was in, the other so ruthless in her determination to revenge herself on her rival. The pure white dove was in the clutches of this relentless hawk, who, while watching her victim so closely, was meditating as to the best means of carrying out her plans.

"Oh, it is horrible!" I murmured, turning pale with emotion.

"Hush!" whispered Beltrami with a sinister look; "she will fall into her own pit."

What did he mean by these strange words? I could not understand; but I had no time nor desire to ask for an explanation, as the terrible drama being played out in the next room riveted my attention; so, with a violent effort of self-repression, I resumed my post of observation, and listened to the conversation between the two actresses in the tragedy. It was idle and frivolous, the conversation of two strangers who had nothing to talk about but the merest commonplace; but this frivolity had for us a ghastly meaning; this commonplace concealed a frightful intention.

"And so, Signora Pallanza, you have never heard your husband mention my name!"

"No, Madame!"

"It is strange," said the Marchesa, smiling; "for in Rome I did what I could to help him in his profession. Eh! yes. I heard him singing Faust at the Apollo, and told all my friends to go and hear the New Mario."

"That is what they call him here, Signora," replied Bianca proudly; "but, indeed, it was kind of you to aid him. I wonder Guiseppe never spoke to me about you, for he never forgets a kindness."

"Ah! I'm afraid some men have not much gratitude," said Madame Beltrami with a laugh. "Never mind, when Signor Pallanza comes in you will see he has not forgotten me."

"He could hardly do that, Madame," answered Bianca, looking with honest admiration at the splendid beauty of the woman before her. "Had I seen you before I would always have remembered you! But—it is so strange!"

"What is strange, Signora?"

"I do not recognize your face, and yet I seem to have heard your voice before."

"Possibly!" said the Marchesa indifferently. "I go about a good deal."

"Were you ever in Verona?"

Madame Beltrami was startled for the moment at this apparently innocent question, but recovered her self-possession in a moment, and laughed gaily in a rather forced fashion,—

"Yes, Signora! I lived there a long time with my first husband, Count Giorgio Morone."

"Morone!" cried Bianca, starting to her feet with a cry of alarm. "Oh! Madame, do you know that palace?"

The Marchesa saw that she had made a mistake by mentioning that fatal name, but with iron nerve opened a fan she had hanging to her girdle and fanned herself slowly.

"Of course I do," she answered quietly; "it belongs to the family of my late husband, and is said to be haunted."

Bianca shivered.

"So it is! so it is!" she muttered in a fearful tone. "I have been in that room. Signor Hugo took me there."

"Signor Hugo!" repeated the Marchesa reflectively.

"I think I have heard my husband speak of that gentleman. He is English, is he not?"

"Yes, Madame. A great friend of my husband's. A terrible thing happened to Guiseppe at Verona! Oh! a terrible thing. And that room, that fearful room! Dio! I shall never forget it."

"You are trembling, Signora! You are ill," cried Madame Beltrami, rising to her feet and crossing quickly to the table before the curtain behind which we were concealed. "Let me give you some wine."

"No, no! thank you. I am quite well!" said Bianca, going to the window and opening it. "It is only the heat. The fresh air will do me good."

"A glass of wine will be better," replied the Marchesa, pouring out a glass of Chianti.

I felt myself seized with a kind of vertigo at seeing this demon take from her breast a small bottle and empty the whole contents of it into the glass. I would have cried out only the voice of Bianca arrested me,—

"I am perfectly well, Madame; but will you not take some wine yourself, since the day is so warm?"

"Certainly, if you will drink with me!" said Madame Beltrami, turning round with a calm smile; "but indeed the wine will do you good, you seem to faint."

She poured out another glass of the Chianti for herself, and was about to take the fatal drink to Bianca, when the latter called quickly from the window,—

"Madame! quick! come here! Guiseppe is coming down the street!"

Out of courtesy the Marchesa was forced to obey the call of her hostess, and went quickly to the window, leaving the two wine-glasses close together on the table, the one on the left containing the poison destined for Bianca, the other on the right innocent of any drug, which she intended to drink herself.

At this moment, while the two women were looking out of the window, I heard the voice of Beltrami, hoarse and broken, sound in my ear,—

"Go to the door and tell the servant to detain Pallanza!"

I looked at him in astonishment, for there was a frightful look of agitation in his pale face, and great drops of sweat were standing on his brow; but he made an imperative gesture, and I obeyed him without a word.

Petronella was in the kitchen, and I hurriedly told her to keep Pallanza at the door on some pretext or another, and stole quickly back to the room, where I found Beltrami leaning against the wall with a haggard look on his face.

"What is the matter?" I whispered quickly. "Are you ill?"

"No, no! Look!—look!—see! See what she is doing!"

I had only been gone a little over two minutes between the time I had last looked in the room and the moment I resumed my post of observation, but during that period the Marchesa, evidently afraid of the entrance of Pallanza, had given Bianca the fatal wine, and the girl was drinking it at the window. Madame Beltrami herself, with rather a pale face, but a devilish look in her eyes, had just set down her glass upon the table, empty. A moment after Bianca, having drained the fatal draught to the dregs, came across to the table and placed her glass beside that of the Marchesa's with a merry laugh.

"I am glad you persuaded me to have the wine, Signora. It is so refreshing."

"Yes, I think you will find it so," replied the Marchesa, with a strange smile.

The whole of this terrible scene had passed so rapidly that I had no time to interfere. My tongue clove to the roof of my mouth, as I saw Bianca drink the Borgian wine; yet with a mighty effort I was about to cry out, when Beltrami seized my arm in his powerful grasp, and dared me, with lurid eyes, to utter a sound.

The Marchesa, having completed her devilish work, was about to go, for I heard her say something to Bianca about seeing Pallanza on the stairs, when suddenly we heard Guiseppe's gay voice talking to Petronella, who strove to detain him; but with a merry laugh he brushed past her, and a moment afterwards was in the room. Standing there in the grasp of Beltrami, hidden by the curtains, there seemed to be a silence lasting an eternity; then we heard Guiseppe give a terrible cry of rage and fear, and despair,—

"Giulietta! you here! Demon! what are you doing?"

Slow and soft, like the hiss of a snake, came the answer,—

"Doing to her what I did to you."

"Poison! Bianca!"

The poor girl gave a terrible shriek of agony, and flung herself into the arms of her husband, while again there sounded the wicked laugh of the Marchesa.

"Ah! you cannot save her now, traitor! perjurer that you are! she will die!"

There was a sudden smash of glass, as Beltrami hurled himself through the archway and stood before his terrible wife.

"You lie, wretch! Here is the antidote!"

Bianca was lying unconscious in Guiseppe's arms, and he, with a cry of joy, stretched out his hand for the phial which Beltrami, standing midway between his wife and the tenor, was holding. Suddenly, with a shriek of rage, the Marchesa sprang forward, and tearing the phial from his hand, hurled it through the open window into the street.

"No, no! She shall die! She shall die!"

I shall never forget that supreme moment of anguish. Bianca lying pale as a lily in the arms of her agonized husband; myself standing amid the ruins of the table in the archway; the Marchesa erect, defiant, and snarling like an enraged tigress; and only Beltrami calm—

Beltrami standing cold and inflexible, with folded arms and a sinister smile on his thin lips. The whole of this frightful drama had only lasted a few minutes, but the denouement, more terrible than anything that had gone before, had now arrived.

"She shall die!" repeated the Marchesa with devilish persistency.

Beltrami gave a wild laugh that sounded like the mocking merriment of a fiend,—

"Fool! you have thrown away your life!"

Guiseppe looked up with sudden hope, and the Marchesa with a cry of abject terror reeled back with staring eyes and outstretched arms as the truth flashed across her mind.

"Life! life! oh! devil that you are, you—you—have changed—"

The fierce beauty of her face was suddenly distorted by a spasm of agony. She put her hands to her throat and tore open her dress, tore off the ruby necklace, the gems of which flashed down to the floor like a rain of blood, then with a yell of fear which had nothing human in its despair, she fell at our feet—dead.

Yes, she had fallen into her own pit; she had flung away her only chance of life in her desire to doom her rival and there amid the brilliant sunshine, amid the blood-red jewels scattered around her, with all her crimes, devilries, and wickedness on her head, lay the dead body of that Creature of the Night I had seen issue like a vampire from the old sepulchre to fulfil her evil destiny; and over her with folded arms, sinister and cruel, towered the man who, as the instrument of God, had sent her back to the hell from whence she had emerged.

***

CHAPTER XVIII

A LAST WORD

It was at the Paris Opera House that I last saw Beltrami, three years after the death of that terrible woman. Things had gone exceedingly well with me since my student life in Milan, and I can say without vanity that Signor Hugo Urbino holds a very good position among operatic artists of to-day. After leaving Angello I devoted another year to hard study, and was finally pronounced fit to appear before an Italian audience by my last Maestro. This, however, was only half the battle, for now, having gained complete control of my vocal powers, I had to take lessons in scena from Maestro Biagio, or, in other words, I had to study the art of acting. I elected to make my début in the fine part of Renato in Verdi's opera, "Un Ballo in Maschera," and having learned the music thoroughly, Biagio taught me how to render the character, dramatically speaking. This took some time, as every movement, every action, every gesture had to be studied; but with perseverance I overcame all difficulties, and at length found myself capable of rendering the character of Renato in a sufficiently good style. In passing I may say that, as far as I have found, it is ridiculous to think that acting comes instinctively. No doubt a histrionic genius is able to give a gesture or strike an attitude during the emotion engendered by the performance of a part, but he must always hold himself well under control, and, broadly speaking, act the character, as he studied it, in cold blood. Otherwise, carried away by his powers, he would do things likely to upset the entire mechanism of the scene. I have sung the part of Renato many times since my first appearance, and the critics are pleased to consider it a striking performance, but whatever touches on the spur of the moment I have introduced, the broad rendering of the character always remains precisely the same as taught to me by Maestro Biagio.

Being thus in a position to sing and act the part, my greatest difficulties commenced, and I can safely say that I never met a more unscrupulous set of scoundrels than these sixth-rate impresarios who go about Milan, like degraded Satans, seeking whom they may devour. English students, being popularly supposed to be made of money, are their favourite victims, and they demand from these the sum of four or five hundred francs as the price of a scrittura, **i.e.**, an appearance on the stage. In a playful, ironical fashion they call this sum a present, I suppose after the fashion of Henry VIII.—I think it was that king— who dubbed his taxes "Benevolences;" and if you do not make the impresario "a present," you certainly will not get an appearance in Italy. With this money they take a theatre in a small town and put on the opera in which you desire to sing, but even then it is doubtful whether the débût so dearly purchased will come off at all.

The first impresario with whom I had to deal was a dingy individual, who, according to his own account, had brought out all the greatest singers of Europe for the last twenty years, and, having made him "a present" of two hundred francs—he was a modest man and asked no more—it was arranged that I should make my débût at Como but on arriving there for rehearsals I found that both the present and the impresario had vanished, like Macbeth's witches, into thin air. Considerably disheartened by this sample of Italian honesty, I yet had sufficient faith to trust another gentleman in the same fashion, but he must have been a brother of the first impresario, for he too vanished. I now began to perceive that there were still brigands in Italy, but that having become civilised, they were either hotel-keepers or impresarios, and as my two unfortunate attempts to get a scrittura had ended in disaster, I was not very anxious to make any one a third "present."

However, it was no use turning back when within the sight of the goal, so I consulted Maestro Biagio, who kindly interested himself on my behalf, and introduced me to an honest impresario, who required the necessary present, but nevertheless fulfilled his promise of introducing me to the Italian public. I made my début at Brescia with great success, and at the conclusion of the season, for which, of course, I did not receive a penny, I had plenty of offers from all parts of the Continent. To make a long story short, I sang everywhere I possibly could, and, having secured an excellent reputation, by an unexpected stroke of good fortune I was engaged to sing at the Paris Opera House two years after my débût. I think Dame Fortune was anxious to make reparation to Hugo Urbino for the misfortunes of Hugh Cranston, for, to my great delight, I was favourably received by the critical Parisians, and before the season ended was overwhelmed with offers of lucrative engagements.

What with my good fortune and the constant excitement of the life of an artiste, I had almost forgotten the episode of Verona when I was reminded of it by the unexpected appearance of Luigi Beltrami, who came to my dressing-room one night at the conclusion of "Il Barbiere," in which I had been singing the part of Figaro.

He was changed, this cynical Marchese, since I had last seen him, and changed for the better, as he had lost his former sinister air and looked much happier and brighter than formerly. Since our parting in Milan he had written me frequently, but of late his letters ceased, so I was somewhat puzzled how to account for this new air of cheerfulness. However, we shook hands heartily, being glad to see one another, and Beltrami, lighting one of his eternal cigarettes, sat down to wait until I was ready to leave the theatre.

"Eh! Hugo," he said, gaily blowing a cloud of smoke, "so things have gone well with you, mon ami?"

"Exceedingly well, Beltrami, or you would not see me in this room."

"Bene! I congratulate you."

"Many thanks, Marchese; but you look as if life were agreeing with you."

Beltrami laughed, not with his former sardonic merriment, but with a hearty sense of enjoyment.

"Ma foi, yes! I am married again!"

"Oh! I hope I can congratulate you this time," I said with great significance.

"The present Marchesa is an angel, mon ami. Dame! I had enough of demons with the Contessa Morone."

"Well, she was punished for her sins."

"Eh! what would you? There is a God, mon ami, and He was wearied of the crimes of that Lucrezia Borgia. But what about the poor girl she tried to poison?"

"Signora Pallanza! Oh, I hear she is in America with her husband. He has made a wonderful success in New York, and Bianca tells me they have two children, a boy and a girl."

"A new Mario and Patti, I suppose. Diavolo! what a pity the old Maestro is not alive to train the voices of his great-grandchildren!"

"Yes, he is dead, poor old man! I heard all about it in Vienna, and Petronella has gone to America to look after her beloved piccola. Well, Angello had a long life, but he was not immortal."

"Dame! perhaps his system is immortal. It ought to be if your singing is an example."

"Ah, flatterer!"

"No; upon my word your Figaro was delightful. It is such a relief to hear a voice without that awful tremolo. But come, are you ready? I want you to sup with me."

"I will be delighted, Beltrami. Is the Marchesa in Paris?"

"Eh! no, not this time. I am here **en garçon** for a few days. Madame is in Florence, where you must come and visit us. We are wonderfully happy. Dame! who wouldn't be with health, wealth, and an angel of a wife? Ecco!"

"You inherited the wealth of Madame Morone?"

"Ma foi! yes. It was the only good turn she ever did me."

"Oh!" I cried, with a revulsion of feeling, "you are becoming cynical again."

"I always become cynical when I think of that demon."

"Beltrami," I said after a pause, as we left the Opera House, "there is a question I have often wished to ask you."

I felt the Marchese's arm tremble a little in mine, but he laughed in a nonchalant manner.

"Eh! ask what you will, mon ami."

"Did you put your hand through the curtains and change the position of those glasses?"

Beltrami stopped and looked at me steadily with a grave look in his bright eyes.

"Hugo, mon ami," he said slowly, "I neither deny nor affirm, what you say. Giulietta Morone was a demon who came into the world to work evil, and God, wearied of her crimes, sent her back to the hell from whence she came. I am not much given to religion, Hugo, as you know, but I believe in a God; and whosoever He chose as an instrument to destroy that which He permitted to exist, rest assured that such a one will be held guiltless for executing the just decree of Heaven!"

He ceased speaking, and we walked on in silence through the crowded streets under the dark-blue summer sky. I understood perfectly what he meant, and whether it was right or wrong it is not for me to say, still I firmly believe that this man obeyed his impulse at that terrible time, not from any selfish motive, but because he saw clearly that in removing this frightful creature from the world he was doing a service to the humanity upon which she preyed.

All the same, I do not intend to visit the Marchese Beltrami at his Florentine palazzo.

FINIS.

BOOKS PUBLISHED BY
PHAROS BOOKS

BOOKS PUBLISHED BY **PHAROS BOOKS**

 sales@pharosbooks.in   011 40395855    www.pharosbooks.in

Plot No.-63, 1st Floor, Main Mother Dairy Road, Pandav Nagar, Delhi-110092